A SNEAKY INC. SPY ADVENTURE

OPERATIØN
ZERO DAY

BOOK 5

A 10 - 16 CHRISTIAN SPY ACTION-ADVENTURE!

CHRISTIAN
ACTION BOOKS
FOR UPPER MIDDLE
GRADE & TEENS

ROB BADDORF

SELAH

God reigns over the nations;
   God is seated on his holy throne.
   Psalm 47:8 (NIV)

———

But you, Lord, sit enthroned forever;
   your renown endures through all generations.
   Psalm 102:12 (NIV)

———

No one will be able to stand against you all the days of your life. As I was with Moses, so I will be with you; *I will never leave you nor forsake you.*
   Joshua 1:5 (NIV)

1

"Um, we've got a problem," Robin whispered, entering from the back of the empty grocery store. He marched forward, holding out his phone.

The gang huddled inside near the lone desk positioned in the center. The Sneaky Inc. hideout. Was this really the kind of place other government agencies met in secret? Didn't they at least have coffee? Hot chocolate?! The team needed to take the time to fix the place up. Fighting with the leaking roof. The leaves that blew in through the cracks and deteriorating walls and were now collecting in the corners. These were ongoing issues.

"Problem?" Chad said, without even looking up.

Why were they inside on such a beautiful day? And all sitting around staring at their phones?

"Anyone want to guess who just texted?" Robin asked.

No one answered.

Or even glanced his way.

Until Isabella offered a huge sigh and slapped her phone facedown on the desk. "I don't get it, Robin." She looked frustrated. "You actually want to sell the food truck? I thought we were all in agreement when we bought it! Sure, there are still a few issues with it, but I thought it was working out for us. Clearly, you don't agree. But do we actually sit around and discuss it as a group? No. You just go and list it on Facebook Marketplace!"

Chad was the next in line to vent his emotions. "And since when do you think using skateboards is unprofessional?! Seriously? You and I've been skating since—I don't know when, first grade? You're welcome to sell all *your* gear, but I'm keeping mine. I used my own money for it, despite how tempting it was to use my department budget now and then on small parts!"

Robin shook his head.

This was all wrong.

A mean-spirited joke Robin wasn't a part of that was now driving a wedge between him and the group.

Or was that the intention?

"And wait," Anika said, sitting up. "You're gonna tell us that none of these messages are actually from you? Because I'll be honest—I know what you said about not wanting to fire me, but I'm starting to get nervous again."

"Did you ever wonder how Zero Day knows so much about our team?" Robin said, strolling around the desk in a wide arc. "How one person could get so much information about each one of us, and so quickly use it against us?"

"Hold on." Isabella adjusted her seat. "You figured it out? You know who Zero Day is?"

2

"For real?" Chad chirped. "I'd love to hear just how hard that was to track down."

"Go ahead and see for yourselves," Robin said, stopping his circling. "Why don't you ask it?."

For a moment, no one moved.

"You're joking," Isabella murmured. Her hand reached for her phone. Only, she hesitated, like it might bite.

Robin dragged a cheap folding chair closer and sat. "You might be surprised by just how straightforward it is. It has nothing to hide, apparently."

Grabbing her phone, Isabella hovered her face in front of it.

BINK.

With a swipe up, she tapped the microphone in the bottom corner of her text app.

She caught Robin's eye. "Who is this? Who are you really?"

Three dots.

"My name is hardly important," a surprisingly human-sounding voice said. It almost came across like a child's voice. A young male? "But some call me Zero Day." And why was it whispering? Almost like the person didn't want his parents to hear the conversation. "I don't see why I should be punished. It's unfair. I only like to have a little fun now and then, that's all. It's not like I'm really hurting anyone."

Eyebrows shot up all around.

Isabella tapped the microphone button again. "Who—who is punishing you, Zero Day?"

"I . . . I really shouldn't be talking about this," the boy's voice said. "Because you never know when they are listening. Ha, that was a joke. You get it?! Huh, huh? Because when it comes to technology, they are always—"

HSSSSSS!

A loud burst of static suddenly interrupted, causing everyone to jump back.

"Pardon me for that," a fresh voice said. It sounded female. Smooth and calm. An adult tone. "I'm sorry for that malfunction. Please note that the Zero Day bug report has already been submitted to the coding team. Thank you. Please note, my general programming is still undergoing final certification. As beta software, I may still experience a few flaws in my coding."

There were only more screwed-up expressions around the desk.

Questions and no answers.

It was Robin's turn to lean in to the phone. He pressed the microphone button. "Thank you for that. And do tell everyone here—who is this now speaking?"

"I am Spark," the voice said cheerfully. "A user-friendly artificial intelligence created by the creative team at Luminous Data. Your digital ally for a better tomorrow!"

2

obin watched the response from his teammates.

"That is *so* freaky!" Anika exclaimed. "No wonder Damien wanted to destroy it. That sounded like the beginning of the end!"

"Yeah," Isabella said, quickly shutting off her phone. She shivered. "And I hope I'm *not* going to keep hearing that voice in my head. Ugh! Now I'm going to have dreams with that in it."

"Artificial intelligence?" Chad grunted. "You've got to be kidding me! And this one has a split personality? That's great. Just what the world needs. Makes you wonder how many more personalities are inside it fighting to get out."

A silence lay over the group.

It all felt so heavy.

Insane!

When Robin heard the whisper. A question.

Who is on the throne?

It was loud enough that Robin spun back around. Had any of them heard it too?

But from the looks on their faces, they were still lost in thought. Chitchatting among themselves. Trying to comprehend the extent of annoyance—or worse—that Zero Day had already caused them.

Robin assumed the whisper's question was rhetorical. That it didn't need an answer.

But just in case . . .

He wandered over to the only display case still in use. Despite the deli glass needing a good cleaning, a collection of staplers sat on display. Of all the luxuries other FBI teams had in their offices, likely none of them had such a fine collection of gothic design and simplicity in the art of securing multiple sheets of paper together.

Robin glanced up at the ceiling. "You alone are on the throne," he whispered.

And waited.

Was there more to the question?

More to come after giving the answer?

Like a buzzer for getting it right.

Or a beam of light about to shine down on him?

But there was nothing.

No other whispers.

No other words.

————

Inside the food truck, Robin selected his utility belt from off the rack. Already wearing his dark-colored, tight-fitting uniform, he slung the belt around his back and latched it around his waist. One side at a time, he tugged the shoulder straps on the belt into place. Then, still one at a time, he selected tools from off the shelf, clipping each into place.

It was time to have a little chat about Spark with someone. Someone who really knew what was going on.

A chance to go deeper into understanding its capabilities. Its threat.

And Bruce Bena, the CEO of Luminous Data, was the man.

Maybe the guy in charge could shed some light on his own software.

And since knocking on the front door of Luminous Data to schedule an appointment with the man would likely get Robin nowhere, he had another idea in mind.

Bruce had just undergone gallbladder surgery. For all Robin knew, the man might appreciate some flowers. Maybe even a lovely get-well card. As Bruce Bena convalesced at his mansion home!

Robin grabbed his backpack and slung it onto his back. "You ready, Chad?"

He glanced outside the food truck where his friend was.

Only, Chad didn't look ready.

If anything, Chad didn't look like he could stand very well, either.

The boy was jumping about, hopping on one leg, trying to pull on his shoe.

"Did you even think about untying them since the last time you wore them?"

"Untie them?!" Chad growled, hopping around, trying to keep his balance. "Do you know how much time an average human loses over the course of their entire life-time," he grunted, breathing heavily, "just tying their shoes?!"

"Um, no." Robin shook his head and ducked around to the other side of the truck.

The girls wore ratty old coveralls and already had a good portion of a second coat on the side of the vehicle. White paint. Pristine. Rolled out to perfection!

"That looks nice," Robin said, pausing to admire their work.

"Yeah, thanks," Anika said, blowing a tight strand of curls away from her face. It had little effect and the curls merely flopped back in place. She finally just grabbed the ornery strand and yanked it behind an ear. Only now, Anika had a streak of white through her hair. "Don't forget, if you get bored and want to come back and brush some, we always have more rollers for you!"

K-THUNK, FLAP. K-THUNK, FLAP.

Chad rounded the corner. He walked with only one shoe on correctly. His heel crushed the back of the other shoe, which hung on little better than a slipper. "Alright, I'm ready. Let's go."

"You sure?" Robin used his head to gesture to his friend's feet.

"Yeah, this sorta thing happens all the time," Chad said casually. "My foot will eventually slide inside it when it's good and ready."

———

The agreement was to no longer use text messaging. At least within the group. With Spark hacking into their accounts, they simply could no longer believe what they were reading.

That meant everything had to move to voice communication.

And sometimes voice was *not* a good option.

Such as when silence was a better option. Or the only option!

Like exactly at that moment.

As Robin and Chad huddled together.

One practically on top of the other.

Hiding behind a much-too-small bush!

Neither one of them moved.

Frozen stiff.

Desperately hoping that the security guard out on patrol would not see them.

Perhaps this had not been the best approach to Bruce Bena's mansion. It seemed right at the time, but Robin was second-guessing everything in the moment.

They had approached the mansion from the rear. Through a large, well-manicured Italian garden. Apparently, it was a replica of a famous one in Italy somewhere.

For some reason, it had looked easy from the satellite photos. Less so in person.

The guard wore a midtone gray uniform and ball cap. Unmarked. No logos or insignias. Likely an outside security firm for hire. He carried a standard-issue M16 rifle and thankfully gave more attention to the Greek fountain statue that was peeing in the pond.

The pink and white figures were all marble.

Little gleeful cherubs.

Chubby and naked. All except for the occasional stone fig leaf.

Striding along the long gravel path, the guard was nearing their hiding spot.

Only a few more seconds and—

"You notice," Chad whispered in Robin's ear, "those chunky statues never stop having to go? You think they drank an entire sixty-four-ounce blue raspberry slushy?"

Robin wanted to die. It would be from either Chad's mouth or the terrible cramp that grew in his thigh. He didn't know which. With both eyes clamped shut, he thrust a finger in front of his lips.

"I should know, because I've done it."

The guard strolled to the other side of their bush.

"Not everyone can hold that much inside. It sloshes about. In your guts."

The guard suddenly paused.

And then he turned on the gravel walkway. His boots grinding in the gravel.

Thankfully his back was now to the boys.

But what was the guard doing? He was no longer moving. Was he taking in the sights?!

"I know they aren't real, but that *is* impressive," Chad whispered, adjusting his position. "I have *never* had to go that long." And with that—

Chad stepped out from behind the bush!

Robin blinked.

He wasn't sure if what he was seeing was real—

Or a hallucination.

Chad stretched his legs.

Just behind the guard!

Starting with a few calisthenics.

Jumping jacks—

And then a few toe touches!

3

Was this a plan they had discussed?!

A brilliant way to slip past the guards? That Chad and Robin had thoroughly planned? Mapped out? Schemed up ahead of time to execute at just the right moment?!

Because Robin couldn't remember one.

And he had *no idea* what Chad was actually doing!

Time slowed.

Surreal.

Just as the guard began to turn back around—

Chad kicked up one foot.

His shoe slipped off, somersaulted in the air.

Chad thrust out a hand—

And caught it!

Immediately thrusting the tip of the shoe into the guard's back.

"Don't!" Chad growled in a hoarse whisper, huddling

in close to the man. "Don't make me use this thing or it will get ugly quick!"

The guard froze.

No one moved.

Not until the guard's arms slowly rose above his head.

Chad turned to Robin. "Come on, you can't tell me you've never wanted to do that with a New Balance."

Chad's attention moved back to his captive. "How can you listen to that fountain every day—" he said, plucking the sidearm out of the man's holster. A pistol. And a backup knife. A walkie-talkie. "The splash of all that water —and not have it make you want to go?"

Chad unclipped the shoulder strap of the M16 and held the rifle out for Robin to take.

Robin didn't do anything. Except blink.

Chad shook the rifle impatiently.

Robin came back to reality and grabbed it.

What was he supposed to do with an M16?!

Chad had the guard kneel and put his hands behind his head before Chad began zip-tying the man. "I want you to think about what I just told you," Chad said as he lashed the man's legs together. "Just listen to that gentle sound of the water and see what it does to your bladder."

Robin stepped back. He held the M16 like it was diseased.

Glancing to both sides, Robin marched over toward the fountain. And with no one else around, he yanked the clip from the M16 and flicked out each bullet with a thumb into the water.

Chad clearly needed help. Therapy of some sort. Robin

just didn't know if Chad actually would ever agree to see a counselor. Or who would come out of it the most changed.

Robin looked into the faces of the cherub statues. They looked happy together. Forever playing, frozen in time. Disassembling the rifle enough to yank out the firing pin, Robin tossed it too. With no other good options, he deposited the rifle into the chubby open hands of one of the statues.

By this time, Chad had the guard fully tied up and gagged.

"Can we go now?" Robin asked.

Chad nodded and held up a finger. "One sec." He slipped his shoe on again. Or tried to. It didn't want to fit on his foot. Maybe because the boy simply would *not* untie it!

Robin had to push on. He simply couldn't stand there watching another fight between Chad and his shoe!

———

Isabella grabbed the fine-tipped brush she held clutched between her teeth. Sitting crisscross on the floor in front of the food truck, she guided the tip of her brush around the first headlight in one full movement. Not bad. She paused, leaning back, and touched up little areas here and there.

The food truck didn't need to be perfect.

After all, it was still a rusty clunker underneath it all. The fresh coat of paint didn't change that. It only helped to disguise it.

And white was the perfect choice.

The closest color to invisibility. At least, when it came to vehicles.

Who looked anymore at a bare white van?

It was innocuous.

Easily forgotten.

The only thing better would be a truck that changed colors on command.

The fine-tipped paintbrush stopped.

Mid-stroke.

Isabella tapped the back end of the brush on her chin, lost in thought.

"Anika, do you remember what happened to those video projectors the team had?"

Anika looked up at her. Reaching over, she paused the music they were both listening to. "Which projectors?"

Isabella climbed to her feet. "You remember the Pintero case? Where we needed a window in a room that had no windows."

Anika nodded. "Yeah, now that you remind me, I do." Climbing to her feet, she led Isabella to the grocery store office area. Using both hands, she pulled on the door that read: STAFF ONLY.

The door stuck.

She pulled again, harder this time.

SCREEECH!

The misshapen door grated against the floor and opened.

A few moths flew out. Anika batted them away. "What do you want the projectors for?"

"I wanna try something," Isabella said, breaking through a cobweb with her hand.

The grocery store's former office area was Sneaky Inc.'s official storage space. If they had bought it for a mission and weren't using it anymore, it got stowed away. There wasn't much organization. Just a lot of dust and wooden pallets to keep the boxed-up supplies off the damp floor.

Isabella flipped the light switch on.

Nothing.

She flipped it a few more times.

Still nothing. She pulled out her phone light instead and stepped inside.

There were so many boxes.

So much junk.

Junk that in all likelihood Chad thought was too good to throw out. That boy wouldn't even let them throw out the boxes that their supplies arrived in.

And yet, if the projectors still worked, they would be in there.

Somewhere buried in the front office storage area. As dark and damp as it was.

Now it was only a matter of finding them!

4

obin eyed the distance to the back door. One of many around the mansion. But this one looked more shielded than the others. If his calculations were correct, it would lead into the finished basement. A game room of sorts, from what he could tell by peering through the glass. Using his binoculars, Robin could make out the side of a pool table and what looked like a foosball game. He didn't need to see more to know this was their way in.

Only, a card scanner prevented Robin and Chad from strolling inside.

"You think you can unlock one of those?" Robin whispered, hunched beside a brick retaining wall near the Olympic-sized pool. "Hotwire us inside?"

"I can open any lock made," Chad replied. "It's just a matter of how long you have to wait while I do it."

"Okay, so what are we talking with one of these?"

Robin held up his pair of binoculars toward the keypad. "It looks like a Honeywell 7800."

"Oh, trust me, we have options here. On the longer side of things, I could just open up the plastic cover and let the rain get to it. Usually once water drips in deep enough, it causes things to rust. That thing would fall apart on its own. If you're interested in that option, I'm guessing about ten years. Plus or minus, of course."

Robin lowered the binoculars. He bit his tongue to control himself before speaking. "Thank you. Thank you for that, but I was *hoping* for something on the other side of the spectrum. Something that took less time. Something closer to thirty seconds."

Chad shrugged and unslung his backpack. "You know, don't blame me. I always want to give you options. There are times you complain I don't give you enough choices. Now it's too many." He unzipped his bag and routed around inside without even looking. "Some people aren't as impatient as you are, Robin. I thought maybe you'd wanna try something different for once. But trust me, I understand if you're in a rush. You don't have to defend yourself."

Chad must have found what he was digging around for, because he pulled out a thin sheet of clear plastic. What looked like it could have been originally designed as an overhead transparency. Was this what the Sneaky Inc. equipment budget was going toward these days?

Or had Chad borrowed it from Mr. Cornwell's trash can at school?

Robin tilted his head to examine it better. Sure enough,

there were several upside-down algebra problems on one half of the sheet, all written out in red and blue marker. Half the sheet remained unused.

"The reason I understand your complete lack of patience likely boils down to one thing." Chad droned on with his abstract lesson as he pulled out an aerosol can. "Cats." He shook the can a few times, popped off the lid with a thumb, and sprayed the overhead transparency with a clear liquid.

"Cats? That's the reason for my impatience?"

"Yes and no. They aren't just the basis for *your* problem. They're everyone's problem," Chad said, recapping the can with one hand. The other hand pinched the overhead transparency by one corner. He gently waved it back and forth, occasionally blowing on it.

"Somehow I'm hesitant to have you actually explain any more than you already have," Robin said with one eyebrow raised. "And I'm rather convinced that I'll regret it. But now you have me curious. How exactly are cats the fundamental problem with the world being impatient?"

"The problem is that cats are too cute for humans to handle!" Chad said with a straight face. And then, before Robin could even respond, Chad jumped to his feet and, after glancing left and right, raced toward the security keypad!

With no cover!

And no warning. Not even a simple request to watch his back!

And if that wasn't bad enough, he was running in front of a massive set of bay windows!

21

Chad pressed his back against the brick wall holding the keypad.

"You see, people feel like it's their responsibility to take photos of that kind of cuteness," Chad said, entirely too loudly, his voice carrying across the stretch of lawn. "You see where I'm going with this?"

"Shh!"

"Oh, I think we're way past trying to keep cat videos a secret. Ha! Most of the world watches them routinely." Chad rotated away from his conversation with Robin and applied the transparency sheet over the keypad. He didn't press hard. Just lightly with the back of his hand. Then he rubbed a finger lightly over every key. "If you think about it, it's because of the proliferation of cat videos that people are fundamentally impatient. They can't get enough of them."

Robin looked around in desperation.

Someone had to be within earshot of this absolutely insane conversation!

Why couldn't Chad close his mouth?!

"Will you stop talking and get back here?!" Robin exclaimed.

"You see that?" Chad said, like he was having an everyday, ordinary conversation at a coffee shop or in the hallway at school. He pointed directly at Robin, looking down his finger at him. "You're being impatient again. Cats—I'm telling you!"

And with that—

RIPPP!

Chad yanked off the sheet of transparency. And he

22

didn't seem to be in much of a rush to get back to Robin's hiding spot, either. Instead, he appeared to be out for a stroll. Maybe enjoying the sunshine in the park.

Robin growled.

It was a no-win scenario. If he tried to rush his teammate, he would only be accused of liking cats too much. And if he didn't, there was no way Chad wouldn't be seen. Or worse, set off an alarm!

Instead, he could only watch as Chad strolled the entire way back to Robin, staring at the transparency held up to the light.

And yet, despite the boy's complete lack of self-awareness, no alarms rang.

And no one fired off a shot.

No one even triggered the vault doors surely hidden just under the grass, dropping Chad into a tank of piranhas.

Instead, Chad plopped himself back down on the grass beside Robin and the brick retaining wall.

Robin eyed his friend.

When Robin's father was still alive, had he ever worked with a co-agent?

One this . . . unique?!

"Got some good prints here," Chad said, holding up the transparency sheet so Robin could view it. "You can easily see the clumping of which buttons are pressed. There. There. Oh, and look!" Chad giggled. "I guess it isn't all that surprising that even a high-tech computer CEO will still use 1-2-3-4 as his password!"

5

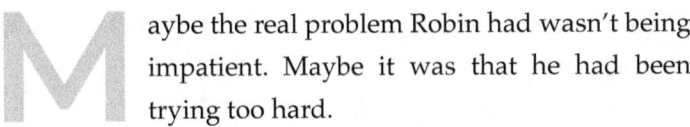aybe the real problem Robin had wasn't being impatient. Maybe it was that he had been trying too hard.

All he had to do was look at Chad's way of life. First with the shoe. Then just now, with the keypad.

Chad seemed to live with a casual, always-at-play sort of attitude. And it seemed to work for him.

Maybe Robin needed to relax more. Play more!

If it worked so well for Chad—

Why wouldn't it work for him?

Robin hesitantly stood. It was less boldly than he wanted to do it, but at least he was up on his feet.

And the important part was that no alarms went off.

Robin took a step out onto the grass. Yes, straight out in the open, heading toward the keypad.

And nothing bad happened.

The sky didn't fall.

The world didn't end.

Robin smiled.

He was emboldened!

Only, when he took the next confident step forward—

BLERTT! BLERTT! BLERTT!

The entire compound burst into panic mode.

Lights blinked!

Alarms blared!

"What did you do?!" Chad yelled.

"I—I didn't do anything!"

Was that true?!

Maybe Chad's unique way of doing things—

Only worked for Chad!

Robin ran. Straight for the basement door. With Chad close behind.

And Robin slammed in the code. 1-2-3-4.

BONK.

The keypad blinked red.

Robin yanked on the door. Still locked!

"I thought you knew the combination!" he growled.

"Oh, I'm sorry," Chad scowled, planting both hands on his hips. "If I'm not mistaken, I thought you ordered the 'Impatient Entry' option. If you'd like a more quality solution, we can always just go back to my first suggestion!"

4-3-2-1.

BONK.

2-3-4-1.

BONK.

Nothing was working!

And the alarms didn't let up either!

They were out of options. Dead in the water!

Robin didn't know what else to do.

What else to try!

What was the mathematical possibility of a four-digit code? Wasn't that four to the fourth power? Two hundred and fifty-six options?!

And then there was always the sickening chance that the code was *more* than four digits. Maybe one of the numbers was used twice.

And those statistics were absolutely mind–blowing!

"You know what?" Chad said rather calmly. "I suppose you could always resort to the *ultimate* impatient option. Since that's likely more your style anyway."

Robin was reaching to type in another combination when he paused. He glanced at Chad.

The boy casually tossed a brick up and down in his hand. Had he pulled that out of the retaining wall?!

Robin offered his lopsided grin. Grabbing the brick, he felt the weight of it. "You're right, this is more my style." And—

SMASH!!

He used it to shatter the glass door!

———

"You want some help looking?" Anika asked.

Isabella didn't respond. She had swapped out her phone light for a small penlight that she now held in her mouth, freeing up both hands to dig through the boxes. Instead, the light moved up and down along with her head nodding.

Anika held up her own penlight and moved to the other side of the storage room.

Squish.

She cringed. Anika had no interest in shining the light on whatever it was she had stepped on.

She had wired the electricity back to the main area of the grocery store, so why hadn't it worked in here? It would have been nice to have some overhead lights again. Anika figured it was just one more thing to add to her growing list of things to fix.

Anika looked around. There were so many boxes. Where should she even start?

The first box she opened spilled over with office blueprints. They hadn't been folded properly. She flipped through a few of them. The office complex on 45th and Progress. Martin Ledger's bank office. Was it worth taking the time to fold them properly now?

Anika closed the box. It was too big of a job to fix everything. Besides, the past was the past. They weren't likely to ever need that stuff again. Right?

She dug around through more boxes.

Replacement doorknobs for a job that had required planting microphones in them at an office complex.

Camera lenses that only worked on thermal cameras.

A box of license plates. From all different states. Unregistered.

Anika's thumb drummed on the side of the box.

An idea!

"Hey, if Spark can use traffic cameras to identify our truck, couldn't we make that more challenging for it?"

Isabella grabbed the penlight out of her mouth. "What are you thinking?"

Anika held up the box of license plates.

When something rattled.

Anika looked down at her box.

The noise hadn't come from the license plates, had it?

It sounded like it had come from somewhere else.

Somewhere between Anika and Isabella.

———

Robin didn't waste time.

He led Chad through the basement.

Past the extensive game room. The ax throwing area. A narrow set of bowling lanes. Two movie theaters—one for larger crowds, the other for smaller, more intimate viewings.

How had the alarm been triggered?

Motion sensors? Or had someone seen Robin approaching the basement door?

If they had, where were they now?

The place was empty. Devoid of humans.

It felt eerie inside. Like it was the staff's day off.

It wasn't adding up.

With Chad close on his tail, Robin approached a set of back stairs. He peered up them.

Clear.

Keeping silent, Robin began taking the steps, one at a time. Heel to toe, preventing his foot from slapping on the bare, polished wood. Always careful to track around him for movement. Above. Below.

And ever listening for other footsteps.

But no one was in this area of the house.

Why not?

Could the sirens be a false alarm? What if they had been activated by another intruder?

It was always possible. But what were the chances?

Robin and Chad worked like one organism. As one of them focused more on what lay ahead, the other constantly protected the rear.

They were in someone else's house.

A house they didn't know except for a few two-dimensional sketches. And none of those displayed things like furniture. Or any installed security systems.

Who knew exactly what might lie—

Around the next corner?

Robin's fist rose up beside him.

Chad froze.

Noise ahead.

Voices.

Where exactly?

Robin and Chad crept up another few steps.

They could hear shouts and yelling from up the next flight of stairs.

Which they took at a snail's pace.

One stair tread.

Then the next.

Hoping none of them would creak.

At last, Robin crested just enough of the staircase to see it.

A standoff. Some distance away.

It involved at least three of the guards. From Robin's vantage point, he could only see their profiles. Several guards knelt in the hallway, their rifles up and at the ready. A handful of staff members were there too, lingering toward the rear. They were all focused elsewhere.

On some activity inside one of the upper rooms.

The double set of polished oak doors to the room lay wide open.

The master bedroom?

And from inside, someone was yelling and screaming.

A series of dreadful and ugly threats!

6

sabella rose to a standing position, holding a set of the video projectors.

They hadn't been as difficult to find as she had imagined. Maybe she had simply gotten lucky opening the correct boxes.

But there was something else that had her attention now.

ZICKA, ZICKA, ZICK.

A rattling sound.

Anika had drawn attention to it with a finger to her lips.

And now Isabella heard it too.

Something was making the nearly imperceptible sound.

Where was it coming from?

It almost sounded like it could have come from one of the many boxes that lay between her and Anika.

When a box off to her side suddenly shook.

Isabella stepped back from it. She clutched the projectors even closer.

Some animal must have bumped it.

A rat?

As much as Isabella had no interest in interacting with the rodent, she wasn't scared of rats. Her grandmother's woodshed was home to plenty of them.

But that still didn't answer the issue of the rattle.

Because as quiet as it was, that sound was coming from a different area of the storage room.

She caught Anika's eye. A look of concern flashed over her friend's face.

They had what they'd come in for, didn't they?

Maybe this was a good time to leave the damp, dark room, before anything else decided to—

Too late!

Another box near the back wall violently rocked side to side.

As if something were inside it.

Desperate to get out!

Aiming straight for the exit, both girls ran!

———

With Chad bringing up the rear, Robin edged forward.

He wanted to see more.

Needed to.

What had triggered the alarms was finally coming together. Robin's step out into the yard hadn't set anything off. And all the noise the brick caused shattering the glass in the door had probably gone unnoticed as well.

The mansion had a bigger problem to deal with.

The one before him down the hallway.

From the snippets of agitated conversation Robin could make out, it sounded like there was an intruder up ahead. One who must have broken into the mansion shortly before Robin and Chad themselves had.

But why?

A common thief?

Clearly, whoever it was had a weapon.

And from their desperate shouts, they were threatening with no uncertainty that they were prepared to use it.

One of the gray-haired staff ladies up ahead stepped closer to the room, framed by the double set of open doors. Both of her hands hovered in front of her, palms outstretched in a sign of peace. She spoke in a clear and calming voice. "Please, we don't want anyone to get hurt. I'm asking you, please set the knife down."

"No! You don't understand!" a voice yelled from some-where inside the room. Male. Angry, if not completely desperate. "I need the money! My kid—he's sick and I can't pay the bills! I have to do this. I have to!"

How much farther could Robin risk inching forward?

Before he became another threat?

Robin frowned. He still wasn't close enough to get a good angle on the room.

"No, you're right," the staff lady said in her serene voice. "I don't understand. But taking Bruce's life won't solve your problems. It will only create more."

"I don't care anymore about *my* life!" the angry voice blurted. "I need the ten million dollars!"

Robin's eyes went wide.

Someone was offering this guy ten million dollars to end Bruce Bena's life?

It had to be Damien Crowe!

He had failed in his attempt on the CEO's life at the hospital.

Now he was trying again.

By bribing others to do his dirty work!

The guy in the room ahead didn't sound like a professional killer. Just the opposite. A desperate man in need of the bribe to help out his kid.

Chad tapped Robin on the shoulder and motioned to another bedroom door closer to them. Chad signaled for them to enter.

Robin nodded and tried the door.

Unlocked.

He cracked it open just far enough for the two of them to slip inside, careful to close it behind themselves.

"I figured there might be a connecting door from this room to the next," Chad whispered, examining the room.

"Good idea." Robin began searching.

It was a bedroom alright. One of the biggest Robin had ever seen. There was so much wasted space between the bed and the dresser that it seemed odd. Robin was used to his own squashed bedroom where, between the clothing on the floor and his single bed, there was hardly any room to walk.

Did anyone really need a bed this big?

What was it? A king-size?

Something larger?!

Even the artwork hanging on the walls looked expensive.

Robin walked into the bathroom. It was just as fancy, with a large marble tub and a walk-in shower with multiple spray heads. It had to be as big as the locker room back at his school.

But there was no connection between the rooms.

Even in the sitting room that presented itself toward the back of the suite, there was only a walk-in closet. As big as his entire living room. Robin scanned inside it. No hidden door.

From all appearances, there was no way to get around behind the intruder.

They needed to find something fast before events next door turned ugly.

Wait, there was something.

Two narrow balcony doors.

Robin pulled on one of them, which opened inward.

But there was no balcony to speak of. At least, not one where you could go out and take in the view or sit and read a book. It was likely better described as a fake balcony. Little more than one foot of space to stand outside on.

Why did they make these? What was the point?

Was it only to let air in?

Robin took the single step out that the balcony would afford him. He glanced both ways.

Sure enough, there was a neighboring balcony where the other bedroom was.

But it too was no wider than his own.

And much too far away to even consider jumping.

"You know, we could try pulling a Tarzan," Chad said, poking his head out too.

"Tarzan?"

"Yeah, you know. Swing on a tree vine. From one balcony to the other."

"Um," Robin said, his eyes narrowing. "I don't happen to see any tree vines, do you?"

"No," Chad said, marching back into the bedroom. He stopped and began pulling something off the giant bed. "But they do have very nice Egyptian cotton bedsheets!"

7

Anika was last to reach the storage room's door.

She burst through the opening without hesitation. She had no need to figure out what was behind her. At least, not until she was out in the open again. In the vast open safety of the empty grocery store.

With some distance between them and the storage room, Anika caught Isabella's eye. "What in . . . the world . . . do you think . . . that was?" she whispered through labored breathing.

Isabella merely shook her head.

"Do you think it could have been a possum? It might have dug its way into a box. Built a home there and we disturbed it."

"I don't know," Isabella whispered. "I suppose it could be. But that doesn't explain the rattling sound."

Both girls stared through the open storage room door.

At the darkness within.

Listening.

Waiting.

Isabella slowly set down the two video projectors on top of the desk.

When Anika glanced down, she was still clutching the box of license plates. She needed to ease up or her fingers would soon ache. With her years of gymnastics skills, Anika gracefully bent her knees and began lowering the box to the floor. But it never made it. Not before—

"Wait," Isabella breathed. "There it is again!"

Both girls froze.

Hunched over, Anika strained to hear better. Willed it!

Holding her breath.

Tilting her head slightly from side to side.

When she did hear it.

As the rattling returned.

Drifting from the storage room.

Anika inched her way back up to fully standing, clutching the box just as tightly as before. "Do we still have the golf clubs in the truck?" she whispered without diverting her gaze from the door.

Isabella's head barely nodded up and down.

As the rattle grew louder.

And louder, until—

THUNK!

The sound of a box falling over inside the storage room echoed out!

Without waiting, both girls spun toward the truck.

Just as the grocery store—

Plunged into darkness!

———

Chad tugged on both sides of the bedsheet. The giant knot in the middle shrank in on itself, tightening. "There, that should be good enough to hold us."

Robin offered a weak smile. "And you're just gonna toss it up in the air and hope something will hold it?"

"You didn't see the dormer window above us? It juts out from the attic. I think our rope is long enough to loop over the peak, don't you?" Chad displayed his long, thick cord of bedsheets as it snaked across the floor.

"Ha! They do this in the movies, Chad. Not in real life!"

Undeterred, Chad marched toward the open balcony again. "You're no fun. This is no different than using my shoe. Come on, it's a classic."

Robin reluctantly followed. Mostly just to see Chad's plan so easily fail. "We don't have time to waste, Chad. This isn't a professional grappling system costing upwards of—"

But with Chad's first throw, one end of the bedsheet surprisingly soared up and over the dormer window. The middle of his makeshift rope lay nicely over the slanted rooftop. As if right on cue, the far end of the bedsheet swung back into Chad's open hand. He knotted it with the other end.

Robin didn't finish his sentence, shaking his head instead.

And he didn't close his mouth as Chad hopped up onto the thin, wobbly railing. "Don't you think you should test it first before you—"

But apparently Chad didn't agree.

That or maybe the kid merely figured that swinging on it over a significant three-story drop into the azaleas was a good enough test.

Because that's just what Chad did!

And it was no small swing either.

How far was it to the other balcony?!

It had to be ten feet at least.

KR-TWANG!

Chad neatly dropped onto the metal railing of the other balcony.

A part of Robin needed to pick up his stomach off the balcony floor. The other part needed to stop the conversation he was having with Chad's parents in his head. The one where he had to explain to them the terrible grief he was feeling about the horrible accident that took their son's life.

"Here, catch," Chad said, swinging the end of the bedsheets back to Robin.

Hold up. Chad didn't actually expect Robin to use it too, did he?!

Yet the bedsheet was already in his face. And his mouth!

Robin grasped for it, barely catching the tail end with a few fingers.

"Go ahead," Chad said. "It's not that big a deal."

Not a big deal, ha.

Robin hesitantly tugged on it. Their makeshift rope stretched a bit. But it felt strong enough to actually work.

Which, despite what his eyes had just taken in, Robin was still skeptical of.

Oh, this did not feel right.

If anything, it felt wrong!

And just to confirm that, Robin looked down over the edge of the railing.

Yes. This *was* wrong.

And there was no doubt about it now!

"God, please cure me of my fear of heights," Robin whispered while he dried his hands off on his pants.

Who's on the throne? came the only response.

The whisper.

"Um, I'm—I'm pretty sure you are," Robin responded as his legs fought against him. He continued to push himself as he climbed up onto the terrifying balcony edge, clutching for handholds in the brick exterior with his fingertips in the process!

Robin needed to focus.

He stared at Chad.

And the opposite balcony.

And the fact that his landing area was at best one foot wide, which did not offer a whole lot of encouragement, but since his friend had just done it successfully there was always the very good chance Robin could do it too, but only if he didn't screw up or maybe even worse, look down!

Robin breathed in. He tried to relax. He needed his brain to stop racing!

It was like gym class. You just had to swing on the thick

rope attached to the ceiling. To clear the gap the gym teacher had mapped out on the floor with jump ropes. It really wasn't any more difficult than that. It was all a game. Just like in gym class. Swinging over the floor of imaginary hot lava.

Right?!

With a last breath, Robin kicked off—

And swung over the great chasm of doom!

8

When the lights were off inside the grocery store—

They were *really* off.

Completely dark.

Like an ink-black nothingness kind of darkness!

After all, the former owners of the grocery store had boarded up all the large windows before they left. The entire wonderful bank of sun-loving windows was long gone!

And Isabella felt the absence.

Especially in her shin. After she tripped over the desk chair!

"OWW!"

She went spreadeagled across the floor, hitting part of an absolutely disgusting puddle with her open mouth!

But she was right back up on her feet.

Spitting out the filthy water.

One arm outstretched before her.

Careful not to collide with any support beams.

Wherever they were!

She really could have taken a moment to pull out her phone.

Or to fish around on the ground for the penlight she dropped.

But those simple things of logic weren't in her mind right then.

It was too focused on something else.

On the dreadful sound that approached them.

TIK, TIK, TIK!

Like little metal feet skittering across the hard tile floor!

The sound started and stopped again.

Isabella didn't really care what the creature was doing. If it was sensing their movements. Or the obstacles in its way.

Isabella only wanted one thing.

A weapon of some kind.

She really wasn't picky.

And they had just the thing.

Inside the food truck. Neatly mounted to the ceiling. A nine iron and maybe a seven. All bought at a yard sale. And for just such an emergency.

But where was the food truck now?

After falling, her orientation—

Was entirely messed up!

Sure, there were cracks of light here and there. In the ceiling. In the walls.

But they offered little in the way of usable illu-mination.

And there was no North Star among them to reorient herself to the room.

The best she had to work with was the sound.

Of the little metal feet.

TIK, TIK, TIK.

And a new sound.

MRR, MRRRR.

Coming from roughly the same direction.

Isabella knew where the sounds had come from. The storage room.

And as long as she was going in the opposite direction—

That was good enough for her!

———

Robin felt the adrenaline rush!

And the wind in his face.

As he swung over the broad expanse.

With his hand and arm muscles working overtime, Robin pulled himself up the bedsheets slightly.

Which was a good thing when it came to having a good grip and not slipping.

But when it came to landing on the other balcony—

It was a bad thing.

Because his swing fell short. Not by much. Just a little.

And that wasn't a critique of his performance. After all, on the gym floor you could get away with being less than perfect. Maybe even dragging one foot in the hot lava and no one would notice.

Not here.

Robin stretched out his foot.

Straining! Reaching!

An inch short.

And despite the eager hands of Chad—

Reaching, grabbing for him—

It didn't work out, mostly because one foot connected with Chad's face.

And Robin went backward. Beginning the long and torturous swing back to his starting place.

"Oh, God!" he cried. "Help me!"

But unless God was *really* working all things out for good—

Physics kicked in.

And Robin's swing back to the original balcony had less umph than his first swing.

Which left him significantly short of his target on the second pass.

And despite reaching his feet out for it—

It only led to more swings.

Back and forth.

Each one lessening more and more.

Until Robin was at a dead standstill. His knuckles pure white.

Somewhere in between the two balconies.

Hanging still over the azaleas three stories below!

9

Anika stepped in it.

Something wet and sticky.

Thicklike. Goopy.

What?!

As long as it wasn't part of the creatures after them—the things hunting Isabella and her—she didn't care!

Anika ran on. Arms outstretched, until—

THUNK!

She hit something large and hard.

And wet.

The food truck!

Her hands ran over the sides of it. Getting perspective on the truck's position. She moved away from the sounds and found the rear of it. With a firm yank, she had both back doors swinging open.

Anika scrambled up into the truck and dropped the box of license plates.

She felt a strong temptation to ram the doors closed behind her.

But Isabella was still out there. Somewhere.

No matter. Anika had work to do. And it was just a little brighter inside the food truck. The bank of computer lights offered some relief. They likely wouldn't last much longer running only on battery backup.

Anika immediately turned to the ceiling.

A series of bungee cords zigzagged back and forth, holding a series of long, skinny items against the ceiling.

Several of which were golf clubs.

Not for sport.

But in case of attack. Lighter and faster than a baseball bat, in a pinch these golf clubs could do some damage.

Including to whatever had just grunted and climbed up onto the back of the food truck!

Wait. It was Isabella!

Anika sighed in relief, tossing her a club.

With both girls inside the truck, they immediately closed the back doors, locking themselves in tight.

"Those are *no* possums or raccoons," Anika whispered. "They sound metallic. Like they're machines or something."

"I agree," Isabella said, shuffling past her. "It's time we find out what they really are. Shed some light on the subject. What do you think?" Isabella plopped herself into the driver's seat and groped around on the dashboard. Somewhere beside the steering wheel, she must have found what she was after and yanked on it.

The food truck headlights blinked on.

High beams too.

It took a second for their eyes to adjust to the brightness.

Then both girls gasped.

———

Robin never liked gym class. Especially the part where you had to climb the rope. He could do it. But not all the way to the ceiling to ring the bell. Few kids could. It was a big deal in the boys' gym class. Either you could go the distance—

Or you couldn't.

Right then, Robin felt inspired. He wanted to go the whole way.

Because despite the fact that there would be little heckling if he couldn't make it—

He didn't like the alternative!

Hand over hand, Robin climbed.

His arm muscles burned. They were already weary from the adrenaline and his aggressive grip. The bedsheets were too slippery for his feet to offer much help. He would have to do this with brute force.

He pushed through the pain!

Higher.

Higher.

Until he couldn't climb any farther. Where the bedsheets stretched up and over the roof of the dormer, he could see they wanted to split apart.

But Robin was high enough now to look in the dormer window.

It was dark and only reflected his own face.

Losing energy, he would have one shot at this. Hoping that a window this high wouldn't be locked, he'd have to let go with one hand and shove it open.

Could he afford to let go?

Since Robin didn't want to be the kid stuck at the edge of the high dive, never quite ready to commit, he did it anyway.

One hand shot out, slapping flat against the glass.

And with his other arm taking his full weight, he shoved the window upward.

To his surprise, it slid up effortlessly.

His free hand immediately gripped the windowsill, quickly joined by the other.

He could do this.

One last pull upward!

And pull he did.

With everything he had. His feet kicking at the bricks. Grunting. Groaning!

His head entered.

And then his upper torso.

Just enough to give his arms a brief rest.

He had made it!

But where was he?

The area was dim.

And not what he was expecting.

Beams of wood stretched out in neat rows.

Sixteen inches apart.

With pink, fluffy cotton candy in between.

No, insulation!

Catching his breath, Robin pulled the rest of himself into the tight attic space. Careful to stay balanced on the narrow two-by-four rafters.

As his eyes adjusted, he could see stacks of boxes closer to the center of the attic. Someone had neatly positioned them atop sheets of plywood, creating a makeshift floor for storage space.

His muscles recovered, Robin straddled the rafters and crawled in the direction of the balcony Chad had successfully landed on. That's where the conflict had been.

And the closer Robin got to that area—

The louder the voices below him became. They were muffled. He couldn't make out individual words.

Yet from the intensity of the yelling below, it sounded like the time for diplomacy was nearing its end.

And like it was time for the guards and their rifles to take over!

The rough wood was painful on his hands and knees.

But Robin pushed himself.

If someone didn't stop things, the situation below would deteriorate quickly.

Except Robin wouldn't have to worry about that.

Not when his hand slipped off the rafter he had just reached for.

Robin's legs and knees went sideways to accommodate his loss of balance—

KR-CRUNCH!

Stabbing through the drywall just below the insulation.

And like a bathtub drain pulling at everything around it—

Robin completely lost it all. His balance, his position, his grip—

CRACKK!

And fell through the ceiling!

10

sabella recoiled and gasped.

It definitely wasn't natural. Not wild animals.

Instead, the headlights reflected off bits of metal and electronics.

As the entire grocery store floor before them seemed to move.

With a sea of the group's very own creations!

Small robots for recording remote conversations.

Drones to patrol the movement of a mark's car.

Four-wheeled remote-controlled vehicles for gaining entrance to a building or facility otherwise off-limits.

Wait!

There was the jumper car that Isabella had created herself! The one she designed to gain entrance to her father's bank office.

There were so many devices Sneaky Inc. had cobbled together.

Mock-ups. Prototypes.

Unfinished experiments that hadn't quite worked out as planned.

Some machines had to drag their incomplete back halves screeching across the flooring.

They were all there!

Approaching the food truck.

Gathering like an army of locusts!

But how? Why?!

Who could have found all these creations buried away in storage? And activated them again into a swarm of machinery?

"Unbelievable," Anika said in awe. "Spark?! Is that what's behind this? If it could hack into our phones, why couldn't it hack into our spare computer parts?"

"Of course." Isabella swallowed hard. "It only makes sense."

"They can't do any actual harm, can they?" Anika asked.

Almost as if on cue, the jumper car's mini-blowtorch rotated outward, snapping into place.

FLLRRRRRR!

A small flame of hot white tipped in blue erupted from it.

Isabella reached for the truck's ignition. "I—I don't think we should stick around long enough to find out." Reaching down, she twisted the vehicle keys.

GRR, RR, RR.

The truck wouldn't start.

GRR, RRRR, RRRR!

The engine still wouldn't catch.

"Please tell me you're *not* doing this as a joke, right?!" Anika groaned, reaching over to lock the passenger door.

Several of the computer-controlled devices were now close enough to the food truck that even when she pressed her head against the window, Isabella couldn't see them anymore.

GRR, RRRRRRRR!

Isabella suddenly let out a long sigh.

Letting her shoulders go limp.

Her head lowered.

As the sound of small metal objects echoed on the outside of the truck.

TAP. TAP. TAP.

Were the machines able to climb the sides of the truck?!

When a flicker of light caught the girls' attention.

It was dim at first.

But quickly grew in intensity.

As flames licked their way up one of the support columns.

And spread to the ceiling!

"I know you don't believe in God," Isabella whispered, reaching out and taking Anika's hand. "But will you pray with me?"

She caught Anika's eye.

Her friend offered a simple nod.

"Please, Lord Jesus. Let this truck start!"

TAP. TAP. TAP.

The flames hungrily consumed one brittle ceiling tile after another. Fragments of ceiling material rained down around them. All on fire!

Isabella twisted the key.

GROWLLLL!

The engine roared to life!

They had *not* opened up the large garage door behind them.

Oh well. It was too late for that now!

Isabella yanked the gear stick into reverse—

And stomped on the gas pedal!

KR-THOOMMM!

They plowed through the garage door backward!

Ripping bits of robots and remote-control vehicles away in the process.

As the food truck, nearly out of control, careened out of the store—

KR-THUNK-UNK!

And down the loading dock ramp!

———

Robin grabbed for whatever he could!

Which wasn't much.

Because after his body plowed through the drywall ceiling—

And through a fancy-looking Tiffany's chandelier—

KR-THOOOFF!

Robin crash-landed square in the center of Bruce Bena's king-size bed!

Eyes wide, Robin shot up into a seated position.

A thin coating of white drywall powder, tufts of pink insolation, and pieces of expensive glass coated him.

With a wild intensity, Robin looked around.

Fortunately, Bruce hadn't been lying in his bed. The patient was perfectly fine, confined to a rolling hospital bed by its side.

As for the knife-wielding attacker—

There was no sign of him.

Only a few groans from the nearby floor.

"Hands up! NOW!" guards yelled, rushing the room.

Robin coughed and immediately complied.

But the guards were more interested in the attacker who had apparently been knocked to the floor. Had the chandelier done that?

"Nice work," someone whispered nearby.

With his hands still up, Robin twisted around to see—

Chad, who was stepping out from behind a pair of thick window curtains. He shot Robin a thumbs-up. "I knew you had a plan!" Chad added with a wink. "The classic chandelier-to-the-head routine!"

11

I t took some convincing to keep the mansion guards from handcuffing Robin and Chad, but in the end, after enough phone calls to FBI headquarters, things were worked out.

"Yes, yes," Chad said, puffing out his chest in front of several uniformed staff members—his adoring fan club, apparently. "We are always glad to help out. As the leader of the group, I like to always be the one to put my life on the line, before anyone else. That just comes with the job, really."

Robin shook his head and, peeling himself away, approached Bruce Bena. The man was still in bed. The CEO of Luminous Data looked pale and a bit out of his element. He still wore a hospital gown. He winced when adjusting his position, which he did sparingly. Various tubes and cables limited his movements and connected him to nearby machines. Despite being in his opulent bedroom, it was the simpler, more humbling machines that were now keeping him alive.

"Excuse me, Mr. Bena," Robin said as he approached the man. "Can I have a word with you?"

Several white-coated doctors attended Bruce. Frowning, they stepped in Robin's way. "No, you may not," one of them said. "Mr. Bena has been through enough already. He needs his rest and cannot talk with anyone right—"

"It's alright," Bruce said, gently shooing aside the doctors. "I can talk with him. After all, he just saved my life. And for the second time, I'm told."

Having cleaned himself off, Robin stepped forward. "Sir, I don't mean to be a bother."

"No, no," Bruce said. "I feel like the least I can do to repay you is provide a few answers."

"Thank you, sir."

"Call me Bruce."

"Alright, Bruce." Robin inched closer to the influential man. "Damien Crowe. I believe this is his second attempt now to kill you."

Bruce winced as he offered a smile. "Ha! Tell him to get in line."

Get in line? Was that a joke?

"I'm sorry," Robin said, "but you might not understand how he motivated the man with the knife today."

"Oh, sadly I do," Bruce said as Chad approached at last, joining the conversation. "I know exactly who was behind this. And who it is that has now invited the entire Internet to hunt me down. Who has offered a ten-million-dollar bounty on my head!" Bruce interrupted himself with a coughing fit.

"If it wasn't Damien Crowe," Chad asked, "then who?"

"Unfortunately, I know what it was like for Doctor Frankenstein." Bruce took another sip of water. "My own creation has turned on me. Spark wants me out of the way. Dead. It wants to take control."

Bruce's words struck like a hammer.

Robin reeled.

What he was hearing sounded like a work of fiction. Fantasy! And yet, Robin had experimented with AI. The early versions of it, anyway. He had sampled its incredible power when he was outlining a paper for civics class. It was amazing, the potential it had. What else was it capable of? And how soon would it break out from its facade of service?!

"There were warning signs," Bruce lamented. "But I ignored them. Told my software developers they were simply paranoid. I wanted to push the outer limits of what science could give me. I stole fire from the gods. And for my sins, I've become a prisoner in my own home."

Robin heard an odd sound beside him.

Like a spoon scraping a bowl.

He glanced to his side, just enough to see Chad finishing up Bruce's bowl of green Jell-O.

Robin closed his eyes. He needed to focus. "But is there anything we can do to stop it? Before *everyone* comes knocking on your front door looking for the ten million dollars? Before Spark takes over completely?"

Bruce leaned over the side of his hospital bed.

Moaning. Coughing!

The doctors all rushed back.

What was happening?

Was the man dying before Robin's very eyes?!

"Help me," Bruce groaned.

Wait. Was he reaching for something?

"Help you?!" Robin blurted, trying to connect the man's eyeline with an object in the room. "Help you with what?!"

Bruce gazed at his bedside table.

A small, ornate, gold-edged table standing on four legs.

Or more specifically, at the drawer in the front of it.

"This?" Robin asked, opening the small drawer. "You want something inside this?!"

Bruce nodded and leaned back, flopping his head onto his pillow. The effort had taken nearly all his energy.

Robin glanced inside the drawer.

A single, somewhat old-fashioned flash drive lay inside.

Robin picked it up like it was the crown jewels themselves.

"Spark is . . . constantly growing. In knowledge . . . understanding . . ." Bruce gasped through labored breathing. "We created a pause button. For if the situation ever turned bad enough. I think we can both agree we're past that now."

Robin nodded.

"Alright, you need to conserve your energy, Mr. Bena," a doctor said, stepping in and taking charge. "This conversation needs to be over. NOW!"

"But—but what do I do with it?!" Robin yelled as he

and Chad were forcibly led away by the doctors and all their staff. "With the flash drive?!"

"Luminous Data," Bruce gasped, coughing up something red. "Plug it in . . . the central server!"

It wasn't much for a set of instructions.

It left out lots of details that would likely get in the way.

Like Spark itself. And everything the AI would throw at Robin and his team to stop them!

But for now—

It was enough!

12

By the time Robin and Chad left, there was a growing army outside. From the looks of things, the police and the National Guard had the perimeter under control, barricading the entire compound. Bruce Bana appeared to be safe, at least for the time being.

Robin drove his car back to the Sneaky Inc. hideout.

An old Toyota Corolla that had seen better days. It was cheap and it ran. That was all. And really, that was all Robin cared about. Maybe he could get a fancy car someday. Something nicer. Without so much rust. But that just didn't seem like a good investment of money. At least, not at this stage of life, anyway.

Chad sat in the passenger seat. Did he actually weigh enough to sit up front? Robin couldn't exactly ask him that without the very real possibility of offending his friend. Technically, with Chad's size and weight being what they were, he was probably supposed to still sit in the back. In one of those goofy booster seats!

Chad contributed bits of food to the already-dirty floor as he chowed down on half a sleeve of saltine crackers.

Robin glanced over.

Watching a steady stream of crumbs dribble out of the wrapper.

"You are planning on vacuuming my entire car when we get back to the hideout, yes?" Robin asked with one eyebrow raised.

"Oh, sure thing," Chad mumbled, pulling a bulky wad of napkins out of his pocket. Unwrapping them, he produced a mostly untouched pork chop and bit into it like a starving dog.

"And you're sure you're not stealing food from a man who is trying to recover from gallbladder surgery?"

Chad shook his head. "I found it on a tray sitting on the floor. It was just outside his door. Bruce had already picked over it." Chad took another bite of what surely was now lukewarm meat. "I didn't want it to go to waste."

"Very thoughtful of you."

Chad nodded.

Robin was going to say more, but he stopped himself as they turned at the next intersection.

Distracted instead by a column of black smoke reaching high into the sky.

Where was that coming from?

And why, despite every turn, were they continuing to head straight for it?!

Even Chad stopped gnawing on the bone.

As red and blue lights swirled up ahead.

Fire trucks.

In the middle of what looked like nowhere.

Near a long-abandoned grocery store.

Or what used to be one.

———

Robin and Chad parked the car some distance away.

And walked toward the smoldering remains of the old grocery store. *Their* store. Their headquarters.

At least three fire trucks had parked on the side of the unused road, jamming it up for any other traffic. Which was next to none.

Police cars too.

One ambulance.

Robin picked up the pace. He was desperate to find out if the girls were okay.

When he heard a whistle.

Robin and Chad paused, looking around.

It had come from up the road a bit. A turnoff for an old logging road. Someone had parked a food truck in the narrow open area before a chain stretched across the dirt road barred further access.

Stepping out from beside the truck, Isabella and Anika offered subdued waves. What had happened to them?! Both were streaked in white paint. Across their clothing and skin, in the most unusual fashion.

Robin changed directions and walked toward them.

But not before he got a good view of their hideout.

Very little remained standing.

Only a few support beams that had somehow been left untouched.

Everything else lay flattened, blackened to a crisp.

The aging avocado green and white tiles could still be seen in a few spots. Ash and rubble covered the rest of the floor.

Several firefighters were wrapping up their hoses and slinging them over their shoulders, carrying them away. With the main fire extinguished, one figure continued to patrol the ruins, laying down a drenching cover for anything that smoldered.

Robin couldn't process it all.

It felt surreal.

Dreamlike.

Laying untouched in the middle of the ruins was a brick. The one that was used to hold up the missing leg on the desk.

The desk—or any part of it—was no longer there.

Only the brick remained.

How many memories had disappeared with the desk?

With the entire place?

An old feeling returned. The cold desperation of loss. The same thing he felt when he lost his father.

"God, I don't understand," Robin whispered. "How . . . how . . ."

Who's on the throne? came the reply.

Robin frowned. He was getting tired of the question. Mostly because he already *knew* the answer. Or thought he did.

But this. This was different!

The wreckage!

The loss!

Their hideout from the beginning. A retreat from the rest of the world.

It wasn't adding up.

Robin shifted his attention as the zebra-striped girls approached. "Is everyone alright?"

Both girls nodded.

"What happened?!" Chad cried, barely able to pull his eyes off the fire trucks.

"Spark," Isabella said coldly.

"Yeah, I get that there was a spark involved in this somewhere. Just look at it!" Chad exclaimed.

"No, not that kind of spark," Anika bit out. "Spark the AI!"

13

Isabella and the group sat in the corner of The Cracked Pot. A local coffee joint that offered amazing chai tea and drizzled lemon scones.

But despite the four steaming cups in front of them—

No one seemed interested in actually enjoying them.

"I don't get it," Robin said with a heaviness over him. "What I don't understand is—"

But Isabella held up a hand, stopping him. Looking around, she leaned over the booth seat, grabbing a small wicker basket off the unused table behind them. She dumped out the crayons, which rolled in every direction across the table, and set the empty basket down among their drinks. "No more talk. Not until everyone unloads their devices. Powered off."

And with that, Isabella took the lead. Tugging on her pants pocket, she slipped out her phone. She shut it off and tossed it into the basket.

One after the other, the entire team followed suit.

Phones.

Smartwatches unstrapped.

A growing pile collected.

"I mean it. Everything!" Isabella growled.

A smart ring.

One Fitbit wristband.

Isabella gave Chad a questioning eye.

"That's it!" he chirped with both hands up. "Seriously, you want to search me? I left my Philips smart lightbulbs at home."

Satisfied, Isabella took the basket up to the front counter. And after a quick dialogue with the barista, the lady kindly tucked their electronics behind the counter.

Isabella marched back, eyeing the ceiling and walls along the way. She paused, doing a double take.

Leaning in toward the wall, she examined a thermostat. She tapped its screen with a fingernail.

Analog.

Old-fashioned. Good!

Isabella finally slid back into her seat.

"Alright now," she whispered. "This may be difficult for us, but we're gonna have to be more careful about what we say and where we talk."

"You think it's really *that* bad?" Robin whispered.

Isabella's eyes narrowed as she stared deep into his. "Do you have any idea how Spark burned down the grocery store? It used our own builds to do it. Everything we had tucked away nicely in storage. Anything that had a computer inside of it or an advanced set of electronics—Spark reanimated them. You should have heard it. All triggered at the same time. Scratching and clawing up and out of the boxes we put them away in. Hunting—tracking Anika and me!"

"I'm sorry," Robin whispered, turning his eyes down.

"I want each of us to think about this," Isabella said in a tone that was intensifying. "If Spark could figure out how to get inside of our phones, enough to send text messages back and forth to each other—" She paused long enough to sip from her drink. "What other information does it have about us, huh?"

"It has our lists of contacts," Anika said.

"Passwords," Robin offered.

Anika sipped her tea. "Account access to every website we've created accounts for."

"Documents. Emails. Our grades."

"Bank accounts."

"Home security systems."

"Not only that," Robin breathed, "but it's in every camera on top of every rooftop, tracking us with facial recognition."

"My Tetris high score!"

"Yes, Chad," Isabella said, "including your Tetris high score. We're so used to giving a computer all kinds of information about ourselves, we don't even think about it anymore. All that personal data, floating around here and there, just waiting for someone smart enough to piece it all together. To bless us with that kind of power—"

"Or destroy us," Robin whispered, falling back against his seat. Then he offered a weak grin, pulling something else from his pocket.

He slid it into the center of the table, where it rotated a few times and eventually came to a stop.

A flash drive.

"Chad and I got this from Bruce Bena. It's the only way to stop Spark. Or at least to put the software on pause for a while. All we have to do is sneak into Luminous Data and—"

"And what?" Isabella said. "Just plug it in?!"

"Um, yeah. That's what Bruce said."

"Do you understand just how wired to the gills a place like Luminous Data is? How much of the latest technology is used in their security system? And what about individual office door access? All key-coded and maintained by none other than—"

"Spark."

"Precisely. It'd be easier to break into Fort Knox or the White House. For all we know, if Spark has already tried to destroy its own maker, then it might already be in control of the entire facility. Reprogrammed all the building passwords. Reworked all the safety protocols. We won't be able to come within ten miles of that place without Spark knowing about it."

"Okay, okay," Chad chimed in. "But let's, just for argument's sake, say we were able to get inside the building. Close enough to shove this flash drive into Spark's belly button. Then what? Isn't it game over? We win?"

Isabella shrugged. "I can only hope that *is* the end of Spark. From what I'm gathering, if Spark is running off of the central servers located inside Luminous Data, then it isn't running anywhere else."

"And how important is that?" Anika asked.

"Very!" Isabella offered a dark laugh. "We can't have Spark escape the building. I've done some reading. Currently, Spark cannot replicate itself like most software. You can't just make a copy of it. That was a safety feature built into its coding. It's vitally important to keep Spark within the building and *then* push the pause button!"

No one talked for a time.

Using one finger, Chad rolled the Cadet Blue crayon back and forth.

Robin leaned in closer. "No wonder Damien Crowe wanted it shut down. And so badly at that. It seems like we're stuck between two criminals this time. A murderous lunatic, ready and capable of throwing the world back into the Dark Ages, and an artificial intelligence with an ugly, dark side. One that it can't seem to control."

"Precisely," Isabella whispered. "A battle of two giants!"

14

obin looked at the time.

It was getting late.

Having lost their hideout and not sure what to do with the food truck, he drove it to the local Walmart. And parked it toward the back of the parking lot.

After disconnecting the powerful computer system inside the food truck from its battery backup and the gasoline generator system, the group locked the truck up tight.

Robin drove them in his Toyota, dropping them off, one at a time. Each to their own home.

Isabella was the last. And after they dropped off Chad, she moved to the front passenger seat.

Robin wasn't sure what to talk about.

Instead, he pushed an ancient technology called a CD into an even more ancient player and watched as it ate the disc. He let the gentle music from the *Fear & Fable* album speak for them both.

Isabella didn't exactly live close to Robin.

Only, it somehow worked out that she was last. Interesting how that kind of thing happened sometimes.

After thoroughly exploring Robin's glove box, Isabella finally broke the silence hovering between them. "You know, it's no surprise that software would eventually show the fingerprint of its makers."

"You mean, the ones who actually coded Spark."

Isabella didn't respond right away. Instead, she drummed the beat of the song on her door handle. "What were we really expecting from all these electronics? In my world of coding, they call it GIGO. Garbage in, garbage out. It only makes sense, then, that a sinful coder can't help but end up putting their own bent worldview—their limited understanding of how everything works—into their own creation. If anything, it's surprising we haven't seen more of it before now."

"I suppose we're the frogs being slowly boiled."

Isabella nodded, gazing out the window as raindrops fell. They both watched as the tears of heaven streaked and smeared across the glass.

Robin glanced at Isabella.

How did he get so lucky?

To have her as a friend?

To have her join the very team he helped to lead?

She was smart. Resourceful under pressure. Creative.

And lovely in so many ways.

Fingerprints from her own maker.

———

BRRT, BRRT!

Robin shot up in bed, breathing fast.

His alarm vibrated on the shelf next to his bed.

He whacked the top of it.

His bedroom and all his belongings surrounded him. The pile of folded blue jeans that still needed a home. A sock shoved between the pages of a Chem2 textbook, acting as a bookmark. Was he supposed to have returned the book before summer break?

He could worry about that later.

Robin was simply glad. Happy to see his room still all in one piece.

He remembered the events of the previous night. The loss of the grocery store.

But it was his dream that disturbed him the most now.

In it, he had been sitting at the desk in their hideout when the fire started. For some reason, the flames erupted from the base of the creaky rolling desk chair. And he had been sitting in it when it happened. He felt the heat underneath. But in the dream, he had been busy writing something important down on the desk. Scribbling with a pencil and paper.

What was he writing?

He couldn't remember. At least in the dream, it had felt important. Urgent. That's the only reason he hadn't simply jumped up from the burning chair.

It had gotten hotter and hotter.

Until Robin couldn't stand it anymore!

Had his father ever been under this sort of pressure?

Brought home this kind of stress from his time in the FBI? If he did, he hid it well.

Why hadn't Robin simply leaped out of the chair?!

He would do that in real life if it came to that, right?

Of course he would.

Why were dreams always so real and so crazy at the same time?

Robin slung his legs out of bed.

His bare feet hitting the floor.

Leaning over, he grabbed a bunched-up towel off the floor.

Only slightly damp.

Good enough.

Robin headed for the bathroom.

Just a silly dream. Nothing more.

Only, a pang of sorrow came over Robin. The real grocery store. It was still gone. The real desk and chair destroyed. Burnt to a crisp.

Where could the group meet now? They had nothing.

He'd have to process that in the shower.

Robin would miss that squeaky chair.

As ratty and stained as it was—

To Robin, that chair had been like home.

15

sabella set her alarm for extra early.

Too early for her! But she really needed to get up.
And now that her cyber life online was flushing down
the toilet, all thanks to an artificial software that was
getting too big for its britches, she had extra work to do.

Isabella glanced at her laptop.

An eyebrow rose. Curious.

Sitting in her chair, she tore a clean sticky note off the
top of the pad. And before powering her laptop on Isabella
flipped the lid open.

In one swift move, she slapped the sticky note over the
little camera lens at the top of the screen. How much could
she trust it hadn't already been on? Recording?

Sure enough, her hunch about something else was
correct.

Three voicemail messages.

Long ago, she had coded her laptop to collect a copy of
every message that arrived on her phone. That way she

could check them whether she had her phone with her or not. Even in study hall.

Her finger dragged over the touch pad.

The first message played:

"Hey, it's Robin. I hope I'm not calling too late. I, ah . . . I just wanted to say I had a good time at The Cracked Pot with you yesterday. I know I'm not supposed to talk about what we talked about there. But I, ah . . . thought maybe if you were available we could talk more. You know, about what I couldn't bring myself to say in the car. But . . . it looks like you're already asleep."

Isabella smiled. The voice was spot on. One hundred percent Robin.

Only, she *knew* that it wasn't Robin.

"No worries," the voice message continued. "Don't feel like you need to call me back or anything, since we need to stay all hush-hush. I get it. I don't know. I guess I just called to hear your voice."

Isabella wanted to laugh. She wasn't an idiot. She knew what was behind some of Robin's longer looks. So did the AI. But she also knew that Robin was a professional. That he would never combine work and pleasure.

That and the fact he was *way* too nervous to ever call her in real life and say anything half as sweet as something like that. If only.

Spark *was* getting smarter!

Imitating the voices of others. Making prank calls.

Letting loose the little foxes so they could run wild and ruin the vineyard. To create confusion among the team!

Isabella had heard it all before.

Her grandmother had even received a phone call from Isabella once. Claiming Isabella had gotten a flat tire along the highway. That she desperately needed money, if only her grandmother could transfer it right away.

Thankfully, her grandmother hung up. Then without hesitation she called Isabella, who happened to be tanning in her own backyard.

Such wickedness!

Pure evil!

Isabella flicked her finger until the mouse pointer hovered over the trash button beside the message. She hesitated. It really was tempting to keep it. A message she would likely never actually receive.

Who knew what else Spark might do to embarrass them?

It would only make things way more awkward if it ever got the chance. Best to be rid of the message now.

Isabella clicked the trash button.

She listened to the two other messages. One from her dentist. The other from a friend at school, inviting her to a Friday party.

But now, with an even better understanding of Spark's abilities—

Everything became suspect.

It almost felt like the solid ground underneath her was shifting. Disappearing.

Truth was becoming muddled. Spongy.

Did she dare call the dentist back?

Or was that fake too?

Phishing for information. Credit card numbers. Social

security numbers. Even the little details of life that seemed meaningless to most people. All of it was potential ammunition for a machine. For electronics that never forgot. Never slept. Never did anything but consume data and then sell it to the highest bidder. The more the better!

Isabella grabbed the laptop's power cable and yanked on it.

She had removed the battery some time ago so hackers couldn't power it up remotely. A reality in some cases even when devices were off.

And she watched the screen go from a busy display of information—

To nothing.

Darkness stared back at her.

Her own faint reflection hinted in the glass.

Hopping up, Isabella went through her room. One device after another, unplugging them all. Especially the most innocuous ones, like the family intercom, her smart speaker, and the air purifier that could reorder filters by itself when needed. Even the CO_2 sensor and the little power adapters in the outlets. Those plugs that let her turn an everyday, ordinary lamp into a smart lamp. One that she could turn off by voice while lying in bed.

Such amazing inventions.

Conveniences.

But at what cost?!

Was she going too far with this?

What was the right amount? A healthy boundary?

Couldn't she just as easily swing the pendulum in the

opposite direction? Become a Luddite—someone against technological changes. That's what Damien Crowe was.

But what about the printing press? Wasn't that a good thing?

Maybe not to the monks it replaced, who had copied everything by hand.

What about the combustion engine? Or the automatic coffee maker downstairs?

Isabella felt dizzy with questions.

"Dear Lord Jesus, please give me the wisdom to know what is okay to use and what to get rid of. Oh, and the ability to find the narrow path down the middle!" she exclaimed. Then whispered, "If it exists."

It might have been a simple prayer, but ever since she started going to church, she felt lost if she didn't give God the problems that were bigger than she could manage on her own.

And now, for some reason, she felt better about it. More at peace.

Her breathing even returning to normal.

Isabella kicked a pair of shorts away that were half-covering her self-steering floor vacuum—

And yanked its charging cord!

16

R obin and the team skateboarded to Walmart and the food truck.

It must have been a big shopping day. The parking lot overflowed with cars. Robin couldn't remember it being this crowded since the holidays last winter.

The food truck looked funny. What might have been the tallest vehicle in the lot, towering above everything else around it.

Robin unlocked the back doors and climbed in. Only, he had forgotten he didn't want to get stuck there. In the back it was difficult to hear anything anyone was saying.

Robin turned around and tried to squeeze out.

Too late.

Chad had already hopped in and now Isabella was climbing in behind him.

"Hold up, Chad," Robin said. "Can I squeeze past?"

The two friends did a little dance. An awkward one.

One where Robin had to sort of go up on his tiptoes while Chad went down into a squat.

Only, they got hung up.

And more than once!

They both backed up and tried passing each other again.

This time Robin went low and Chad went high.

It didn't work.

Robin got a nose full of Chad's underarm at one uncomfortable point. His hair pinched, then pulled.

"Ow!"

"You're standing on my foot!"

"I didn't do it on purpose!"

Not until after what felt like more than Robin's fair share of cruel and unusual punishment—

Did they finally make it. Not until Chad climbed up on the computer station and marched across it. Which, of course, only brought more angry complaints from the rear of the truck.

"Hey! Not with your shoes on!"

"I can't believe it! Do you live in a barn?!"

Now all Robin had to do was squeeze past Isabella.

He swallowed hard.

And decided against it. He was just fine where he was.

"Alright," Robin said, rallying the troops. "We need to get started on studying Luminous Data, to find some kind of entrance into the building without Spark actually seeing us. My hope is—"

"I'm sorry," Anika interrupted from the very back.

"Can everyone move closer to the front? I can't breathe squished against the doors."

Everyone shuffled a bit.

"Good?" Robin asked. "Alright, where was I? My hope is—"

"Hey!" Chad yelled from the front. "Don't do that!"

TINK, TINK.

The sound of metal connecting with metal rang out.

Chad pointed out the passenger window that absolutely no one else had access to. "The kid in the car next to us keeps opening and closing his car door into us!"

TINK, TINK.

"And he isn't stopping, either. I think the little runt might actually be *enjoying* this! Hold on. I'm going out there and giving that three-year-old a piece of my mind!" Chad unlocked the passenger door. "No one messes with our paint job!"

"No!" Robin yelled and immediately regretted it. He quieted his voice. "I mean, it's just a kid, right?"

"Yeah!" Chad growled, rolling up his sleeves. "But it's time he learned a lesson or two about the hard knocks of life!"

Isabella stifled a smile. "Easy there, tiger. His mommy will probably figure out what's going on soon."

And sure enough, the sound stopped.

"Alright, are we all good?" Robin said, a bit frustrated. "My hope is—"

"No!" Chad screamed, leaping for the driver's seat—

Ramming both hands on the center of the steering wheel!

HOOONK!!

Everyone jumped.

Chad leaped back into the passenger seat like a monkey. His face smashed against the side window. He turned away, a look of deep sorrow written across his face. "She stopped him alright," Chad lamented. "She slapped the back of his hand and he burst into tears. Then the mom drove away with her coffee mug still on the roof of her car. Figures."

"Listen!" Robin barked. "I understand this isn't the best location, alright? I get it! But we need to figure out our approach on Luminous Data. And with the grocery store gone, we simply need to make this work!"

"That sounds okay to me," Isabella said, strapping into her seat. "But we're gonna have to do most of our research old-school. I don't trust the computer system anymore."

"Alright, good. Chad, will you give us a drive-by of Luminous Data? We'll see what we can gather with binoculars and thermal cameras."

"Roger that," Chad said, hopping back into the driver's seat. He cranked the engine a few times until it finally caught.

With his foot on the brake, he checked his side mirror. It must have been clear, because Chad tugged the gearshift into reverse—

Drifting back—

SCREETCH!

Only to slam on the brakes again. Everyone lurched with the abrupt stop.

"Oh brother," Robin grumbled, tapping his foot. "What now?!"

"Just our luck." Chad stared into his side mirror. "Here comes the shopping cart retrieval machine. What has to be the longest one I've ever seen, too."

Robin rolled his eyes. "Alright, that's fine. We can be patient."

"Only, now it's just stopped," Anika said, peering through the small back window curtain.

"Fine, I'll deal with it." With a grimace, Robin slipped out the passenger side door. Now outside, he followed the long train of shopping carts—one tucked into the next—looking for the source. And there it was. A red motorized machine behind the parade, capable of pushing such an enormous weight. Except the store employee operating it was nowhere to be seen.

Robin looked left, right.

No worker.

Great.

Just great!

They just had to take their break and leave it right behind the Sneaky Inc. truck—

Completely blocking it in!

17

"Fine!" Robin grunted to himself.

He marched back to the cart pusher machine. It couldn't be that difficult to operate. Could it?!

Sure, it looked easy. The controls weren't that involved.

Robin glanced around one more time. And still without seeing any Walmart employees, he shoved the throttle control into forward gear.

To be honest, the machine was fun to drive. If the FBI ever laid Robin off, he would definitely consider this job!

Using the small steering stick, Robin guided the lengthy stack of carts ahead of him. Pushing, shoving the entire snake of carts further forward.

And when the long line was at least one car's distance past the food truck, Robin abandoned it. After all, it was someone else's job. Maybe they had to run to the restroom. Or were helping someone who had locked their keys in their car.

Robin jogged back to the food truck and jumped inside. "Alright, we should be good to go."

Chad eased the truck into reverse, letting it drift backward, when—

SCREETCH!

He braked again. The entire truck surged to a stop.

"What is it NOW?!" Robin yelled, shoving his head out the window to look for himself.

Sure enough, a second row of carts motored up, blocking the truck!

Throwing open the door, Robin stormed out again. He didn't really want to yell at the parking lot employee but this was getting to be a bit much!

Robin rounded the corner of the truck. He took in a deep breath and opened his mouth wide. His canine teeth flashing!

Only, he didn't yell at the employee.

Because there was no one driving the cart pusher machine.

Was it operating on its own?

Robin spun around.

No, it had to be remote control. Could the operator be in front of the store?

That's when a dark thought washed over him.

Much like the whisper. But this was the inverse of that. A coldness that could only mean one thing. One that Robin had little interest in giving his focus to.

He looked upward.

All around him.

Every single parking lot light sported a security camera. So did the upper edges of the building. So many, it was hard to even count them.

Pointing in every angle.

Unblinking.

Robin didn't want to become a conspiracy theorist. But . . .

He ran to the back of the cart pusher. It was the same controls. Feeling his impatience grow, Robin increased the speed. He steered the machine beside the first string of carts. It wasn't exactly helping anyone else out, but that was someone else's problem, right?

With the two rows of carts clear, Robin dusted his hands. He yelled out, "Chad, can you hear me?!"

He saw Anika offer a thumbs-up in the back window.

"Alright, I'll direct you," Robin called. "It's clear. You can back up now."

And the food truck lurched backward again.

More.

More.

It was good, with everything working just fine.

Until it wasn't.

Because someone shoved Robin from behind!

Pushing him toward the approaching food truck!

Robin spun, desperate to get clear. But it wasn't a person.

Together, the two rows of carts created a wall of metal, pushing him back.

"Stop! STOP!"

The food truck brakes squealed.

But the cart pushers didn't stop. They continued to shove Robin further. He tried to scramble up onto the top of the carts, but he didn't make it. Not before they squashed him against the truck!

"UGH!" Robin groaned. He shoved back against the carts. No luck. He didn't have a good angle to push from, and they had too much weight and traction!

Robin cried out again. Losing blood to his head. His vision blurred.

That many carts were crushing him. Stealing his breath!

The pushers' wheels continued to spin, creating a cloud of burnt rubber. The acrid smell bringing tears to his eyes. Unrelenting. Determined.

When the food truck suddenly leaped forward!

Robin could barely stand. He stumbled forward, gasping for breath, as—

CRUNCHH-BANGG!!!

The food truck made a way, breaking free of the parking jam. It plowed through the parked cars. One smaller vehicle flipped onto its side. Others shoved aside like discarded playthings. Metal scraping against asphalt!

The cart pushers continued their steady approach on Robin.

Only, now he had somewhere to go.

Robin struggled to keep his feet.

BUMP, BUMP.

Constantly prodded by the carts behind him.

Robin picked up speed, gaining distance from the machines.

Until he reached out—
And took Anika's hand.
With both back doors swinging side to side—
She lifted him in as the truck sped on!

18

obin lay on the floor.

Taking up the entire narrow walkway. Thankfully, Anika moved up front, into the passenger seat. And with Isabella in her sliding chair, Robin had his own space to recover.

That had been close.

Closer than he liked.

This really was no longer merely a question of how to approach the Luminous Data building, but of how to survive a standard parking lot.

No—it was even bigger than that. How to go about normal life without wondering if the next pencil sharpener was out to get them. Or if the next fast food drive-through might be holding a grudge.

Robin winced, sitting up. "Isabella, will you GPS us a route to Luminous Data that avoids as many security cameras as we can? I want to find the most remote way there. And I don't care how much longer it takes."

Isabella looked down at Robin sympathetically as she unfolded a large sheet of paper. "I'm offline, remember? These old paper maps don't have that kind of information," she said, flattening out the map on her computer table.

Robin groaned and struggled to his feet.

They both examined the spaghetti diagram of their city.

Robin blinked.

Did people actually use these things? And still knew where they were and where they were going? How?!

"I'll be the first to admit it," Isabella said. "I'm rather dependent on my phone's GPS. I use it all the time to get around. I'd hate to go back to the days when you had to use one of these obnoxious-sized maps. I'm not really an expert with them. Any guess where we are?"

Robin didn't have a chance to answer.

SCREETCH!

Because gravitational forces threw him forward, the brakes squealing yet again.

Robin collided with Isabella, who was still strapped to her seat with a four-point harness system.

"Sorry!" Chad yelled from the front. "But it's *not* my fault! I'm telling you, there was no yellow light. It was green one moment and then red the next! And look at this," he continued. "I don't believe it!"

Robin scrambled back to his feet. He was tired of being a punching bag. It felt like most of his muscles were going on strike. "What am I looking at?"

"The traffic lights!" Chad laughed, his thumbs drumming on the steering wheel. "They're *all* green except for our light!"

"What happens if you edge forward?" Robin asked, hunched over. He craned his neck to peer up at the only traffic light hanging above them that indeed shone red.

The food truck inched forward.

But the light didn't change.

HOONNK!

Someone behind them didn't like it. But then again, neither did Robin.

"It's possible the light is out," Robin said. "Wait until it's clear and just switch lanes."

Chad eyed the side mirror.

And as an opening appeared—

He swung the wheel and pulled out.

"STOP!" Anika yelled, bracing against the dashboard. "Now it's red!"

The food truck lurched to a stop again, halfway into the intersection.

HONK! HOONK!

As the cross traffic suddenly began, completely annoyed at the truck blocking their way.

"Put it in reverse!" Robin yelled.

And just as Chad yanked the gear stick out of drive—

HOOONK!

The car behind them got annoyed again. Inching closer to the food truck's bumper.

"What do I do?!" Chad yelled.

Advice came from every direction.

"Put on your hazards!"

"Wait until it's green again!"

"You're blocking traffic!"

And that's when Chad yanked the truck back into drive. And like the madman the kid so often was, he gunned the engine.

SQUEAL!

Burning rubber.

And barely threaded the crisscross traffic!

With everyone in the truck covering their eyes.

Waiting for the collision!

Only, it didn't occur.

Robin honestly couldn't believe it.

He glanced over his shoulder.

Just in time to look through the rear curtains as—

FLOOOF!

There was a flash of bright light high above.

Traffic cameras?!

Robin could hardly comprehend what was happening to them.

"I don't believe that," Anika laughed. "We actually survived?! Will someone pinch me because I still don't believe it."

It was Isabella's turn to laugh. Even Robin joined in!

The laughter brought a sense of relief to their situation. The crazy intersection now behind them.

Not exactly how Robin imagined it.

But safe and sound. And really, that was about all he could hope for. Because getting involved in an accident right then would have been just about the worst thing that—

CRASSHHH!

A vehicle collided with the food truck!

Sideswiping it!

That brought an abrupt seriousness back to the group.

Chad slowed down and put on his turn signal, pulling off to the side. The other vehicle, ahead of them now, did the same.

No one talked.

Robin let the acid in his stomach settle. They could deal with this. Automobile accidents happened every day. That's why they had insurance. And really, it hadn't been all that bad, right? Robin wouldn't know until he climbed out of the truck.

After another awkward passing with Isabella, Robin hopped out the back. He was mentally prepping himself.

But why were his hands shaking?

As the leader, Robin would do the talking. He would try to explain things and exchange the proper contact information and paperwork.

The other driver got out of his car, clearly shaken. A gentleman wearing a light tan suit. He was mostly bald, but what hair he did have was rather disheveled. The man pulled out a comb and worked on fixing it.

And just as Robin went to start the apologies—

"I'm so sorry!" the man said, shaking his head. "I really don't know what happened back there. It's clearly my fault. I just don't get it."

"That's alright," Robin said, trying to force a smile. The last thing he wanted was for the poor guy to be too hard on himself. "No worries. Everyone with me is alright. I'm sure we can figure things out."

Robin glanced back at Chad and Anika through the front windshield. He nodded, shooting them an okay sign.

"I'm so confused," the man said, tugging out his driver's license. "I just bought the BMW semi-autonomous car—what?—a month ago. I guess I'm still learning how it drives itself."

The man held out his driver's license.

But Robin didn't take it.

He was in shock.

Because he watched as the unmanned car put on its blinker. Then the vehicle pulled out onto the road again. Driving away.

By itself.

With the door still wide open!

The man spun around. Horror across his face. "Wait! It can't do that! It's driving without me!" Despite his dress shoes, the man took off running after his own car.

But the BMW was a good distance away already.

A hundred yards. Maybe two.

When it suddenly squealed its tires—

And spun around.

Facing them.

The headlights blinked on.

The businessman's run slowed.

Slower.

Until he stopped, probably trying to understand what his vehicle was doing.

And then the expensive-looking car careened forward—

Racing directly toward them!

19

Robin blinked.

This could not be real. It felt like a dream.

He took a step backward.

Then another.

Surreal.

Half real. Half crazy.

But the BMW wasn't slowing. If anything, it picked up speed!

And after the businessman scurried off the road, leaping over the guardrail—

Robin figured he might want to do something similar.

Yes!

He spun. Sprinted!

Robin jumped for the passenger door as Anika flung it open.

And none too early!

At the last second, Chad swerved. The force threw

Robin further inside. The food truck barely avoided a head-on collision with the BMW but—

CRUNCHH!

Lost the passenger door. Ripped off only inches behind Robin!

The severed door tumbled, dancing on the roadway behind them.

The BMW had passed them when its brake lights flashed red. And then the car began a textbook three-point turn.

"It's coming back!" Isabella yelled as Anika joined her in the back. "Any chance we can get out of here?!"

"Working on it!" Chad growled, pinning the accelerator down.

The engine roared!

The speedometer needle vibrated from intensity. Ever edging upward!

Chad performed his magic behind the wheel. Which usually felt more like madness!

Deftly weaving through traffic.

Threading between orange construction barrels. Smashing through a handful of them!

Yet as the food truck slalomed from lane to lane, Chad doing his best to avoid obstacles for once—

The BMW was gaining on them.

Faster!

Closing the distance between vehicles!

"Chad, get in the right lane up ahead," Robin said. His gaze flitted between the view in front of them and the one out the missing door.

The food truck swerved right.

"Now, I want you to signal for a left turn," Robin whispered, pointing ahead. "And at the last second, take the right."

Chad grinned.

With the truck's left turn signal blinking—

And the BMW nearly on top of them—

Chad waited.

Waited.

Never once tapping the brakes—

And at the last second—

Chad wrenched the steering wheel right!

The Sneaky Inc. food truck groaned. The forces of metal torquing. Rubber sliding!

As the truck powerslid through the intersection, the back end whipping around—

Until the entire truck tipped up onto two wheels!

Chad corrected for the slide. A delicate play with the steering wheel, just as—

KR—KRUNCH!

The food truck righted itself again! The other two wheels slammed back down, bouncing until the truck fixed itself on the ground again. Chad gracefully continued pressing the vehicle onward in its new direction.

But not so for the BMW.

It braked.

Only to lock up the wheels!

And even with its subtle attempt at a last-second turn, it only sent the car spinning.

Out of control!

Through the intersection.

Completely missing the turn.

Careening sideways, it caught the edge of the far curb.

KR-TUNKA-TUNKA-TUNK!

It rolled. Tumbling over and over!

A deadly dance of twisted metal and shattered glass!

When it—

CRUNCHH!

Stopped.

Instantly. Neatly wrapped around a giant oak!

Robin partially hung outside the truck to watch. Only when truly satisfied their pursuer was gone did he lean back inside.

He slumped into the passenger seat.

His shoulders melted.

His entire body begging for a rest!

No one talked for a time.

At least for Robin, he was too shaken.

Disturbed at not only the bizarre situation that had just happened—

But also its reality!

"God," Robin whispered. "Thank you for protecting us. I really don't think we would have survived that without you. But even if we had perished, you are definitely still on the throne!"

Robin laughed.

Where did the joy come from?!

It had bubbled up from deep inside him.

It all seemed too absurd. Almost comical!

Robin eyed the massive hole beside him.

The missing door.

Maybe it was the stress of everything, but Robin thrust an arm out into the passing wind.

And forming a wing with his hand, he let it drift.

Up and down.

Like nothing was wrong.

Just another beautiful summer day.

"I will not fear," he whispered. "Though the earth give way . . . and the mountains fall into the heart of the sea!"

"Hey!" a voice yelled from the back.

Anika!

"I believe I know where we are on the map!" she cheered. "Take a right up ahead, Chad. That'll put us back on Market Street. From there, we can follow it to the other side of the city and Luminous Data."

Everyone cheered!

Sneaky Inc. was finally back in the saddle.

But Robin heard a quiet sound.

THUMPA-THUMPA-THUMPA.

Where was that coming from?

Inside the truck?

Outside?

"Anyone hungry?" Chad chimed in. "I see a McDonald's over there. And there's a Wendy's on the other side. We can always hit both of 'em. Get fries from McDonald's and dip 'em in a Frosty."

"Shh," Robin said, still trying to track the source.

It was quieter when he leaned in toward Chad.

Didn't that mean it was outside?

As Chad pulled the food truck onto Market Street, Robin peered out of the truck, looking forward.

With the wind whipping past, it was even trickier to find the source of the sound.

But Robin still heard it.

A cyclical noise that—hold on!—matched the acceleration of the truck.

With his head still outside the open door, Robin looked backward.

"Ugh."

He found it.

The right rear tire on the truck was going flat!

It was amazing Chad could still drive and not feel the effects of it.

"Pull over!" Robin yelled.

"Are you serious?!" Chad laughed. "Ooh, we should get Happy Meals instead!"

"No," Robin growled, leaning back inside. He offered Chad his best stern face. "We're not getting Happy Meals. We have a flat tire!"

"Oh, seriously? I thought something felt odd. You know, that might have been a world record."

"Pull in there," Robin said, pointing ahead. "And what might be a world record?"

Chad flicked on his turn signal. "How many people have actually put a food truck up on two wheels, huh? Do you think we can call Guinness?"

Chad pulled the food truck off the road.

With the McDonald's too far ahead, they turned into a car dealership instead. The place looked closed.

The food truck coasted.

Slowing.

Until it came to a stop. With all the problems they had been having with the starter, Chad left the engine idling.

Robin gripped the handrail beside the door. "This shouldn't take long." And he swung out of the truck.

Ready to get to work! Now, where was the spare tire again? Underneath the truck?

Only, he spied something as he hunched down and looked under their vehicle.

Not something connected to the food truck. But what lay beyond it.

In the car dealership's parking lot sat an all-silver truck.

Futuristic.

Boxy and oddly shaped.

Robin slowly stood.

He turned around, gazing at the lot of cars beside him. Surrounding him.

There was another silver truck.

And another.

Along with more space-age sleek cars.

Cars that had no front grill. Was that because they didn't require cooling in the traditional method?

Robin's stomach sank.

He didn't know if he should run. Or hide!

Glancing up, high into the sky, Robin read the car dealership's sign.

It glowed bright.

TESLA MOTORS.

20

sabella had her head buried in the map.

It was finally making sense.

If Anika hadn't given it a once-over, found her home street on the map, and traced things from there, they might never have found out where they were!

Isabella had been on Market Street loads of times. She and her mom liked to shop there. It was one of the biggest shopping areas around town. But getting there? That was another thing altogether.

Up until recently, her mother had always driven.

And Isabella hadn't watched how to get there.

Why would she?

Especially when she had a phone to entertain her. No, not just to entertain her. To do work with!

A drive was a drive. Why not squeeze in a little coding on the way to Hobby Lobby? Or catch up on a little reading on the way to her favorite clothing store?

Learning how to navigate on a paper map surely wasn't all that difficult.

Why, if she studied it a little more, she probably could—

Robin entered the truck again.

White as a sheet!

Was he ill?

He wasn't going to be sick on the floor of the truck, was he?

"What's wrong?" Isabella said. "Do you need help putting on the spare ti—"

Only, Robin had already lifted a finger.

He placed it ever so gently against his lips.

"You know what?" Chad said, adjusting the side mirror. "Instead of Happy Meals, what do you guys say we get flame-broiled burgers instead? Burger King makes them your way, after all. I could really go for a—"

Robin leaned in close enough to bump heads with Chad. "Drive," he breathed. "Stop. Talking. And. Drive." Robin enunciated each word. Painfully slow and crystal clear.

Unnerved, Chad glanced up at Robin.

From the look on Chad's face, he could tell something was wrong.

"Alright," Chad whispered, nodding. "Fine. No Burger King."

"Slow." Robin whispered. "And steady."

With the truck still running, Chad gently eased down on the brake pedal. And performed what might have been the Guinness World Record for the slowest shift from park into drive.

That's when Isabella began to understand the severity of their situation.

She unbuckled her four-point straps, slowly climbing to her feet. Anika was already at the back glass, pushing aside the window blinds.

What was out there?

Maybe a mugger? A man with a gun who had held Robin up, demanding money?

Only, no criminal was out there.

Nor anyone else, for that matter. Was the dealership closed?

Nothing but a lot overloaded with shiny new cars.

Then Isabella saw the T-shaped logo.

It was tiny. And imprinted on each and every vehicle surrounding them.

This *was* worse.

Much, much worse!

They had jumped out of the frying pan—

Into the fire.

Instinctively, Isabella put a hand to her mouth, stifling a cry. It felt almost as if they were on a frozen lake. Ice cracking and splintering all around them. Ready to break at any moment!

And if Robin didn't throw up—

She would!

The food truck didn't lurch at all. It went from a dead stop to rolling seamlessly. Inch by inch.

No bumps. No sudden jerks. Almost as if a breeze had merely breathed on it.

Nothing but the occasional—

THUMPA.

Of the flat tire making a full circle.

The speedometer didn't register any speed. It simply couldn't detect anything slower than three miles an hour.

And this wasn't even a walking speed.

This was torture!

Passing by one Tesla self-driving car—

After another.

An entire sea of computerized machines. Simple means of transportation in the hands of humans. Potential weapons of mass destruction in the grips of a computer!

And the distance they still had to go? Staggering!

Until they did it.

The Sneaky Inc. truck rolled undetected to the far side of the car lot.

Passing by all the featured deals.

"New Models!" the sign displayed. "Now Smarter!"

A necessary journey to reach the other exit!

———

Robin stared through the front windshield.

But he again couldn't believe what he was seeing.

They had plastered the car dealership with security systems. Cameras. Motion sensors. Pressure plates in the ground. The designers of the car dealership had set it up like a bank.

There was no way Sneaky Inc. was getting anywhere undetected!

Could the entire security system be on its own private network?

Disconnected from the rest of the world?

A blank spot in the unblinking gaze of Spark?!

It sure felt that way.

Drifting as slowly as they were.

Barely making ground any better than a snail.

A hundred feet to go—that was it. Then they'd be back out on Market Street. If the girls had indeed figured out where they were on the map, that meant they could navigate on their own. And from there, they could take back roads. Get off the beaten path. Away from the eyes of the machines.

Once clear, they could stop and fix the flat. But not before then. They would drive on the rim of the wheel if they had to—maybe even destroying it in the process!

Robin glanced over at Chad.

The boy had sweat running down his face. He was blinking away the stinging salt.

Robin fared little better. He wanted to yell. At Chad. At the world! He desperately wanted the truck to speed up. But they couldn't. Shouldn't! Because what they were doing was working!

Yet it meant Robin had nothing to do. No way to help.

He wanted the driver's seat for himself. To have the steering wheel between *his* fingers.

Robin could barely stand it!

He *wanted* control!

THUMPA.

An eternity passed before—

THUMPA.

The last seventy feet.

Fifty.

With nothing stopping them—

Thirty.

Or even trying to!

Ten feet.

Chad eased on the brake, bringing the truck to a stop before the exit. He looked left to see if the traffic was clear to pull out.

Three cars, all in a line, were passing by.

The food truck would have to wait.

Only seconds more.

A bump.

Robin felt it. Subtle.

Had something gently moved the truck?!

And just then the last car out on Market Street passed by, leaving a huge gap before any more traffic was even in sight.

"Okay, it's clear," Robin whispered. "Go, now! Floor it!"

Leaning into it, Chad stomped his leg down!

GROOOARR!

The engine growled, racing at a high speed!

But despite engaging all the power the truck had—

It went nowhere!

"What are you doing?!" Robin yelled.

"I'm giving it everything it has!" Chad let off the gas, then stomped on it again.

The engine growled again. Fierce and angry!
Only, this time they at least went somewhere.
Slowly drifting backward!

21

obin's eyes shot wide.

What was happening? It didn't make sense.

He had leaned over and double-checked it himself. Chad had the truck in drive. Drive meant forward. Only, they weren't going forward!

Grabbing the handle beside the missing door, Robin leaned out.

With an all-wheel truck, the front wheels spun like crazy. And with the correct rotation: forward.

But the wheels were no longer touching the ground!

Robin rotated his head.

The same was true of the rear wheels.

What was holding them?!

Leaning out as far as he could, Robin peered under the truck.

A flat, bright yellow device was holding them. Robin had seen the device before. An automated guided vehicle. Or AGV, as they were commonly called. They were built to move around autonomously, to pick up large crates or even vehicles and move them. Amazon used them all over their warehouses. And even car dealerships were beginning to get wise to their uses. Imagine the power of going home at night and in the morning finding that your entire lot of cars had been rearranged to follow new market trends. Or of shuffling lower-selling vehicles to the front for a quick one-day sale. All the labor done for you by machines!

And here their food truck was being hauled by just such an AGV. It must have followed them and slid under just before they tried to exit the lot.

And now it was dragging them backward. Toward the center of the dealership!

Robin pulled himself back inside the truck. "Rock it!" he yelled. "Rock the truck, back and forth, as hard as you can!"

It was tricky to get everyone inside leaning in the same direction.

But they did it!

And the truck teetered. Slowly at first. Then more and more. The rocking movement grew in intensity.

"Back and forth!" Robin commanded. In unison, he and the girls ran from the front of the truck to the back. All while Chad gunned the engine!

The belongings inside the truck clattered and banged into each other, creating all sorts of racket. But the group's efforts had the desired effect.

The front wheels connected to the ground again, gaining grip for a moment.

Then the back wheels, squealing against the asphalt, when—

KR-THUNK!

Their truck caught a break, driving up and over the lumpy AGV!

"GO, GO, GO!" Robin yelled, thrusting his finger forward.

Chad didn't need instructions.

He once more gave the truck all it had!

The truck leaped forward. Gaining speed. Momentum. And yet—

The Tesla cars closest to the exit drifted toward one another. Barring the way!

And like a wave, the next set of cars closed the gap.

Then the next.

And glancing out the door, Robin spied the entire car lot doing the same thing behind them.

Vehicles forming a wall of metal.

Blocking any and all exits!

Chad slammed on the brakes. The food truck groaned to a full stop.

Yet the driverless cars didn't stop.

They continued to close in.

Tighter.

And tighter, until—

CRASH!

One of the self-driving cars collided with them. It sent shockwaves through the truck.

CRASH! CRASHH! CRASHHH!

Now from every angle. Every direction!

The food truck took a beating!

As a dozen different vehicles rammed into it, backing up only to ram it again!

The corners started to invert, the truck caving in on itself!

The battered vehicle threw Robin and the others this way and that. Taking the abuse for them!

Chad scrambled out of the driver's seat. He crawled toward the middle.

PSSSH! PSSSH!

The glass inside the food truck exploded!

"Save the equipment!" Isabella yelled over the din of twisting metal. "Grab anything you can!"

Robin shook his head. "It's too late! We have to get out of here!"

But how?!

Despite the thrashing, Robin looked up. "Lord, will you help us?"

And he saw it!

No time to be gentle. Robin jumped up onto the narrow computer desk. His foot crunching against a keyboard. He shoved open the rooftop vent. And gripping both edges of the opening, he pulled himself up and out. But it wasn't easy. Like trying to climb out of a paint can while it was still in the shaker!

Robin scrambled out onto the roof. He reached down to take the next hand.

Anika climbed out, followed by Chad.

Only, Isabella hadn't held out her hand yet.

"What are you waiting for?!" Robin yelled down through the hatch.

"I can't—I can't leave it," Isabella lamented, trying to steady herself. She looked lost in thought as her computer equipment was being shaken apart. Destroyed before her eyes. "It's everything I own. I can't lose it!"

CRASH! CRASHH!

Robin lay down on the roof of the food truck, getting closer to her. He could feel the flat metal underneath him warp and bend. With his face inside the vent hole, Robin's voice quieted. "I'm so sorry, Isabella." Despite the violent shaking, he lowered a steady hand.

And with a tear sliding down her cheek—

Isabella reached up and took hold.

22

"Here!" Chad pointed, keeping his center of gravity low on the roof of what remained of the food truck. "Over here—one of the cars has already beaten itself to death. We can get out!"

Robin nodded to Chad as he and Anika lifted Isabella up and out of the ventilation hatch.

Chad tried to time it between vehicle strikes.

Then he jumped!

THUNK!

Onto a neighboring motionless car, denting the roof as he landed. And from there, Chad leaped from one car to the next. The other vehicles were all boxed in and had no room to move. It wasn't difficult to make progress.

Anika followed the same path as Chad. She gracefully leaped from roof to roof. A ballet of sorts over top of a packed field of vehicles.

"You go next," Robin instructed Isabella. They didn't have long before there would be nothing left of the food truck. He encouraged Isabella toward the edge but he didn't rush her.

Isabella's eyes suddenly went wide.

"The flash drive!" she blurted. "I left it inside the center drawer! I have to go back!"

Robin shook his head. "You go. I'll get it!" He hesitated just enough to make sure Isabella landed on top of the nearest defunct car. Then, turning to the ceiling hatch, Robin dove headfirst—

Back inside!

It was dark.

Most of the windows and openings for the lights had caved in on themselves already. He almost didn't recognize the insides of their truck anymore. Everything had shifted. Or mashed together, forming new shapes.

There was little room left to stand. Robin nearly tripped on something.

He reached down, only to lift the steering wheel. Severed clean through.

How had it gotten back there?!

Robin felt for the computer desk. But it wasn't where it was supposed to be. He felt around in the dark, running his fingers over everything in front of him.

"Ouch!" Jagged metal.

The vehicles outside battering the food truck did not relent.

He only had seconds to find it.

Before the flash drive would become a permanent part of the truck!

There! Was that it?!

Robin yanked open the drawer. Or tried to. Bent, it didn't want to slide out. Robin tried again. No-go. It wouldn't budge more than the first inch.

"God, give me the strength of Samson, I pray."

Gritting his teeth, Robin gripped the drawer one more time. Giving it everything he had, he forced it to open. Grunting and groaning in the process! And sure enough, the metal scraped against itself, resisting. But it opened. Just enough for him to slip a hand into.

He had it!

And after tucking the flash drive into a pocket, Robin jumped upward. He used Isabella's wide-screen monitor as a foothold and climbed through the ventilation hatch.

Only, the opening had warped. Slowly bending itself closed.

Robin clawed. Grasped for a handhold he just couldn't find.

Sucking in his gut.

Breathing out all his air.

Just to squeeze through—

The shrinking hole!

And he did.

Had someone nudged him from below?!

Robin leaped.

As the wreckage that once was the official Sneaky Inc. mobile command center tilted to one side and toppled over!

Now, with the food truck out of commission, the self-directed vehicles turned to the cars around it. Battering them too!

Robin danced.

From one vehicle's rooftop—

THUNK-UNK!

To the next. He didn't even have time to strategize. Or to direct his path.

Robin instinctively jumped. A few times back to the previous vehicle, as they were all shuffling about now. Detangling. Reorganizing themselves as a cohesive whole.

But it was too late for the vehicles.

Robin took his last leap—

Grabbing hold of a string of colorful triangle flags hanging overhead—

And he swung off the pack of angry cars—

Into the arms of his friends!

And before any vehicles could disentangle themselves enough to give chase—

The Sneaky Inc. team ran!

23

obin's lungs burned. But he wouldn't let up.

Pressing on. Always on the run.

Right now, he could have been enjoying his summer break. A day at the public swimming pool. Out for a hike around Wildwood Lake.

Even wrapping sheets of Burger Barn wax paper around juicy beef patties. What was so wrong about doing that? It had been an honest job. Sure, it might not have paid well, but what did that really matter?

Robin was second-guessing everything. What was he doing?!

He honestly had no idea anymore.

The group clung together, their pace only slowing a little. And even then, pausing just long enough to catch their breath.

The only rule they were holding to was no roads. Only the yards of houses and areas with plenty of trees. Robin wanted the option to dodge behind something substantial in case a car came out of nowhere.

And yet, there was some debate on exactly where they were headed.

They had no hideout to return to.

And Luminous Data felt like an infinity away. Across town. And for what? Just a view of the building? They hadn't even been prepared to enter it. No, something that complicated usually took a week or two of heavy surveillance. And right now, they couldn't even pull that off!

Robin didn't want to be the one to say it . . . but they were lost.

No one had thought to grab the paper map. And with the danger of being tracked, they had all agreed to leave their cell phones at home. Was that a mistake? Robin felt naked without his. Without the GPS features it so kindly offered. Without a way to contact his FBI handlers.

Robin had never felt more alone.

Abandoned.

Robin slipped out from between a row of townhouses. There were no street cameras here. Just a kid riding circles with his kick scooter. And a girl drawing with chalk on the sidewalk.

"Hey, anyone have a water bottle?" Chad asked. "I'm dying of thirst."

Anika shook her head. "I could use a drink too. Can we stop somewhere and buy something?"

Robin frowned. He didn't like the idea of going into a store. Who knew what kind of security systems they had running? But Robin felt the pangs of thirst too. He had for the better part of the last hour, but he didn't want to say anything. Likely the same with the girls.

Not seeing any cars, he stepped forward, keeping his head low. He held a hand beside his face, shielding it from at least one direction. He needed to look casual. Not draw attention to himself. Like nothing was out of the ordinary.

Robin glanced left. Right.

Clear.

No cars approached.

He motioned for the others to cross after him. And in single file, they followed suit.

Yet Robin could feel it.

Boiling inside.

Somewhere deep in his gut.

An anger.

A mounting resentment.

Why had Spark singled out Sneaky Inc. for such torment? Likely because of their involvement with the federal government and positions of authority. It wouldn't have taken a computer long to figure that out.

But Sneaky Inc. wasn't anything special, were they? Not really. Just another FBI team working behind the scenes. Usually assigned to some of the most boring missions. Jobs that were well beneath their capabilities. They had only gotten lucky once—with Marlin Ledger. And who could have known just how personal that mission would become for the group when they took it.

Trying to out-mastermind Spark wasn't even a proper

mission. Not for a set of teen recruits. This was too much. A mission way over their heads!

They were dealing with something completely different. Out of control!

A destroyer of worlds.

What acted like a god among men.

Robin scouted ahead again. A small deli store stood on the corner. Nothing more than a mom-and-pop store with a homemade sign.

Their advertised discounts on two-liter bottles looked faded. Sun-bleached. This would do. Just the kind of place to get off the streets again and get lost inside.

They would have to risk it if they were going any further.

The team entered with the tinkle of a little bell as the front door opened.

The inside was even better than Robin had imagined. Uneven floors. Stained linoleum. It looked like a place out of the past. From a time that was simpler.

No one stood behind the front counter.

A blocky, old-fashioned TV played in the corner. Tinfoil stretched between two antennas. Local news played on the screen, muted.

And the cash register stood completely unguarded. A small note taped to the front of it read: BACK IN FIVE.

They were safe here.

At least, for a while.

Until they got some energy back and could ask for directions. If anyone still worked here, that was.

The store wasn't big. The team split up, taking different aisles.

Robin wasn't looking for anything in particular. He just needed the chance to stop moving. The opportunity to give his leg muscles a break.

Robin found himself in an odd section. It displayed firewood for sale on the same shelf as Sterno fuel cans for camping, baby formula, little tree-shaped car air fresheners, and a travel-size checkers board game. From the design on the game's packaging, it looked to be left over from another century.

Robin smiled again.

Maybe the entire world wasn't falling apart.

At least, not like the high-tech part of it appeared to be.

"Hey," Chad said, ducking his head into Robin's aisle. "They have a buy one, get one deal on Mary Jane candies. You wanna go in on it together and split the whole container?"

"Mary Jane candies? What are they?"

"Oh, you don't know about Mary Janes? They're made with real molasses and peanut butter!"

"Ahh, that sounds gross," Robin said, wrinkling his nose. "No thanks."

"Alrighty then, that's more for me!" Chad squealed as he disappeared again.

24

The girls milled past Robin. They each carried half-gallon jugs of iced tea mixed with lemonade. A good portion of their drinks was already gone.

And that's when Robin spied it.

After he had picked up a waffle iron to examine.

A lone object stood behind it. A thin layer of dust lay overtop.

No way. He had seen one of these before. At his grandparents' house. A long, long time ago!

Robin gingerly picked it up.

A small, square robot with a windup knob on the side of it. The toy wasn't very big. It could easily fit in Robin's hand.

Putting the waffle iron back, Robin twisted the knob. It made a pleasing noise.

Then Robin set the robot back down on the metal shelf.

The toy teetered from side to side. With one foot rotating in front of the other, the robot actually walked. It wasn't fast. At best, a quarter of an inch forward with each step. But it was fun!

Robin leaned in. The robot looked almost hand-painted. Designed in a different era when likely the toymaker could only guess at what those machines would actually look like someday.

Robin picked up the toy again. Without the challenging work of walking, the legs rattled and moved much quicker, vibrating in his hand. Then, as the windup knob eventually stopped, so did the robot.

Robin flipped the toy over.

A faded sticker said: 75 CENTS.

Was that for real?!

DING-A-LING.

The bell on the front door rang again.

Chad began talking to someone. Whoever it was sounded friendly. Likely the owner of the store returning.

Clutching the robot, Robin marched toward the front. He would buy it. If for no other reason than it gave him a smile.

And smiles were in short supply these days.

Sure enough, Chad had what looked like a twenty-pound plastic container of Mary Janes already up on the counter. He was fishing through his wallet and pulled out a twenty dollar bill.

Behind the cash register stood an elderly lady. White hair. A kind and wrinkled face. She wore what looked like one sweater on top of another. All that on a summer day?

The cashier took Chad's money and didn't bother to actually count the candy. She told him they might be a little old—possibly past the sell-by date already. But she insisted she would give Chad a good deal on them. And five dollars for the entire container did seem to be a good deal.

Chad's smile stretched from ear to ear.

The girls weren't ready to check out yet. Saying something about finding a slide-top freezer in the back with popsicles.

Robin was next in line. He approached, setting the windup toy on the counter.

And reached into his pocket as he dug around for his cash.

"Oh, I have no idea where you found this little guy," the old lady said. "But I'm glad to see it's finding a new home."

Robin smiled.

But only half-heartedly. He couldn't find his cash.

Had he left it at home?

So just like he had a thousand times before in his life—

He pulled out his debit card instead.

And without even thinking—

He tapped it against the reader.

Only after it offered a simple, cheerful sound—

BING.

Did he regret it.

His entire world slowed.

No. Was it too late?!

Could he push the cancel button? Stop the purchase?

All without the data traveling over a million miles of electrical cables?!

And a thousand computer processors?!

"Um . . ." was all Robin could manage to say. He was frozen in fear. As the elderly lady put his tiny toy in a small paper bag, folded over the top edge neatly, and handed it to him.

"We really need to go!" Robin yelled to the girls in the back as he shoved the bag into a pants pocket.

Their faces suddenly appeared. With a wide selection of ice cream novelties between them. Seeing Robin's face, their smiles faltered.

"I—I might have made a mistake," Robin breathed.

25

The race to pay the old lady for everything was on.

Chad wanted to give the lady a hundred dollar bill to cover everything and simply get out of there.

But the old lady wouldn't hear of it. And with some of the food already open and consumed, they couldn't put it back.

And when someone suggested that any leftover money could be a tip—

The lady firmly stated that she took no charity!

Robin felt sick.

It had been such an easy mistake.

Nothing that drew attention to itself ordinarily.

How many times had he used the card throughout his life already?

Countless!

Finally receiving their change, hands shoved bills and

coins into whatever pockets they reached first. It didn't matter.

They simply had to go.

And as fast as humanly possible!

Finally—

DING, -ING -ING.

Sounded the front door as Robin and the girls raced through it.

Only to find Chad ten feet in front of them.

Oddly enough, both of his hands were over his head.

His container of Mary Janes lay at his feet, broken. Candy scattered on the sidewalk before him.

Chad didn't move.

Not even a little. Which, for Chad, was saying a lot!

Robin's eyes finally registered.

What clearly was holding Chad at bay.

A semicircle of figures. Dressed all in black. Half of them stood while the others knelt some distance away. Kevlar helmets and balaclava masks. Thick vests. Combat boots. M4 carbine rifles aimed and ready. None of them moved.

Or even blinked!

Four letters emblazoned in crisp white told Robin all he needed to know.

SWAT.

"Stop where you are!" came a commanding voice from somewhere behind Robin. "Slowly put your hands over your heads. And I mean SLOWLY!"

Ice cream sandwiches dropped.

Drinks abandoned—

GLUG, GLUG.

Emptying themselves onto the warm summer sidewalk.

———

Isabella never had a record.

Not until now, at least.

If nothing else, it was completely humiliating.

They had been swatted. And by none other than a "concerned citizen" who wanted to remain anonymous.

That's how Spark had spun it.

It made up some story about a threat to homeland security. The word *terrorists* was used in there somewhere. A pure fabrication. But it was enough to call the professionals out.

It took several more hours before the SWAT officers would even consider unlocking the handcuffs. And by then, Isabella and the others all had severe chafing on their wrists.

Then there were the holding cells.

Did they purposely keep the lights low? Making the place feel cold and dim? Everything Isabella touched was metal. Hard and lifeless. Perfectly conditioned to suck the heat out of everything.

The girls were in one cell. The boys in the neighboring one. With bars separating them.

For the most part the group sat in silence.

No one had anything to say.

Just regret. And that went without saying. Instead, they simply wallowed in it. And much like the holding cell itself, there was no warmth in the regret.

Robin was likely taking most of the blame. Beating himself up quietly.

From her hard bench seat, Isabella watched him.

Watched as his face soured. Twisted and grew hard. His usual joyful spirit and playfulness melted away completely.

Isabella couldn't blame him. If there ever were a temptation to quit, this was it. She didn't know what to do. Likely none of them did.

All her skills in computers and technology now worked against her. Isabella didn't have anything else to offer the team. She couldn't even read a map!

And as if they weren't all feeling bad enough already, it took the police forever to contact their FBI handlers. The red tape only got thicker—knee-deep, for a while. All the way up the chain it went. Eventually one congressional representative who was supposed to be on vacation in Maui had to contact another one. He probably wasn't happy about that.

Yet it wasn't the Federal Bureau of Investigation that finally released them.

Apparently, another federal agency got involved.

One that, if Isabella had her way, they never would have interacted with. Not again!

"Hello there, guys," the voice said, entering the outer holding area.

Zeke displayed his badge to the cell guards.

"You all look good behind bars," Mia added after getting her clearance. Of course the girl just had to say that with a smile, didn't she? "I hear you're looking at doing five to ten in a maximum federal prison."

"Unless, of course . . ." Zeke fought off his own grin. "You'd like a little help?"

26

"Hey, don't worry about it," Zeke said, slapping Robin on the back as everyone exited the police station. "I'm sure you would have done it for us if we were in your shoes."

The sun was already long gone. The street lamps hummed overhead. Their sickly yellow light offered a poor replacement.

What did the group have left?

They were without a ride.

Without a hideout. Robin didn't like the spot they were in.

Being without.

Being beholden to others for their help. And in nearly every area!

"You guys have a way out of here, right?" Mia asked.

Chad was the first to speak up. "We did, but it's been pounded into a small ball of metal by now. So, if you're offering a ride, I'm pretty sure none of us would refuse."

Zeke looked at his sister then back to the group. "What do you say we get Chinese takeout and have a talk about some of our mutual friends? Damien Crowe and Spark."

Everything inside of Robin resisted.

There was only one Chinese dish that he liked—Orange Chicken—and he didn't feel like talking about anything right then. Especially not with the competition. But . . .

If God *was* still on the throne, then this must have been what He wanted.

Because Sneaky Inc. really didn't have any other options.

"Alright," Robin shrugged. "Why not?"

———

The CIA drove boring cars.

SUVs, to be exact. And just like Robin had imagined. Black tinted windows, nondescript. A big yawn overall.

But the vehicle apparently did have more going on than one might first see. Chad wouldn't close his mouth during the drive. He asked just about every question that came to his mind.

Like if the engine was souped-up? If the glass was bulletproof?

And according to Zeke and Mia, they were. All of it was true!

A twin-turbocharged 3.4-liter V6. Whatever that meant.

The CIA could even swap out all the vehicle's glass in under an hour. Depending on the armament needed. Zeke proudly stated they had all the options, from acrylic, polycarbonate and glass-clad polycarbonate to insulated ballistic glass and traditional laminated glass.

But Robin wasn't envious.

He just rolled his eyes instead.

Mia called ahead for the food.

A Grubhub driver met them near the entrance to Zeke and Mia's unmarked office. From the number of bags handed over, it looked like they would have plenty of food. And that accounted for Chad too. So, it was saying something.

There was supposed to be an underground parking garage around back. But for the sake of speed, Zeke parked the SUV along the street.

The building itself was tall. A mirrored glass exterior. Just about as boring as their cars. It didn't announce itself. There were no signs labeling it as a federal office space. There simply were no signs of any kind.

And it wasn't until they all climbed into the elevator that things got interesting.

The elevator required biometrics to operate.

An eye scanner!

Robin watched as Mia leaned in close and a wide strip of light passed over her eye. Only then, with an approval message, did the elevator begin to lift.

This whole place was wired. Electronic. High-end security with computers behind it all.

Then why weren't the CIA getting nailed by Spark?!

Why hadn't they met the dark side of the artificial intelligence? Its murderous split personality?!

It seemed unfair.

But of course, that didn't matter. They were CIA, and Robin and his team were FBI. And as long as that clear distinction was established, he didn't care.

The smell of the takeout made Robin's mouth water.

He needed to prepare himself.

For the strong likelihood that they wouldn't have any Orange Chicken. And that he would dislike their office space. Or that he would like it too much!

He could envision it even before they arrived. It would mirror their choice in vehicles and office buildings.

Corporate boring.

A field of cubicles designed to shrink your view of life down to six feet by six feet.

Stuffy conference rooms decorated with modern art. Or what passed as modern art these days—paint splashed on a canvas. Carpets with that strong smell of plastic and chemicals.

It would be an office space mostly decorated with paper shredders. The universal most-necessary tool for erasing things. Conversations. People's histories. Their futures. It didn't matter if it didn't fit in the thin little slot—you could always just shove it in harder!

DING.

And just then, the elevator doors opened.

Onto nothing.

A big, gigantic stretch of nothing.

The stark beauty of it took Robin's breath away.

He wanted to run out into it. To throw out his arms and hug the great big nothing!

But he resisted. Robin didn't want Zeke and Mia to know his feelings.

They stepped out into the great white room. Only a handful of all-white structural pillars were dotted through-out, breaking up the vast space.

And then there were the windows. Stretching from floor to ceiling. Wrapping around the entire space. They offered a nighttime view of the entire city. A million pinpricks of light welcomed him from every direction.

And if that wasn't stunning enough, the waxed floor gave off a fuzzy reflection of the lights. Doubling them!

Mia and Zeke carried the food to the center of the room. To a lone desk that sat in the middle.

It wasn't that Robin hadn't seen it. He had. But being a white desk, it blended in so nicely that he hardly took note of it.

This all seemed too perfect.

Too much like the old grocery store.

But a lot cleaner.

And brighter.

And with a much more stunning view!

"Help yourself to the food," Mia said, pulling out the paper plates, forks, and napkins. "Hopefully there should be enough for everyone."

"Oh," Chad said, clapping his hands. "You might not know it from looking at me, but I'm a big eater!"

Isabella and Anika nodded.

Mia set out the white Chinese food boxes, side by side on the table. "I ordered all different kinds of dishes. And I ordered double of their special tonight," she said, pulling out an extra-large box. "Orange Chicken!"

27

Robin said a silent prayer before digging in.

And did he ever.

It had to be the best Chinese food Robin ever ate!

He was fairly certain being hungry from sitting around for half a day inside a high-security cell helped. Along with all the unusual stress he had been experiencing lately.

Robin helped himself to seconds.

There really was no worry about the food running out. Though Chad did his very best to put a dent in it.

Finally, Robin lay back on the floor. Zeke had carried in white folding chairs from another floor of the building, but Robin hadn't taken one.

He felt full. And for the first time that day, he sighed with contentment. Granted, being a guy, it probably didn't take much.

That's when he remembered something else. The thought of it brought a smile to his face.

He fished about in several velcro pockets until he found it.

His windup robot!

The shiny paint had flaked off in a few areas, showing the metal underneath. He didn't care. After cranking the little knob, he let it loose on the vast open floor.

Rolling over onto his side, he watched it.

It seemed funny. A tiny robot let loose in such an enormous world. It was a toy. It didn't know about the other objects around it. Or the struggles and wars in other places. The hand-painted robot just did its thing—one foot after the other. And likely thought itself victorious for traversing all of three inches in the process!

"Maybe this is working out better than I thought," Zeke said, "with us bumping into you guys again. We've been continuing to track Damien Crowe and his whereabouts. We have leads, but nothing concrete. Although we can guess at his next target: Luminous Data."

Mia chimed in. "But he can't attack it outright. That's because of their iron dome. A missile defense system that will knock anything that approaches it out of the sky. Damien will need to get into the building first, in order to shut down the dome manually. That's why we've already worked out a plan for how to get inside. We want to beat him there and catch him when he goes after Spark."

"Wait!" Isabella blurted. "You already figured out a way inside?!"

"Yes, but then we're stuck," Mia said. "Spark has built up so many self-defense mechanisms, we don't know how to shut it down at the core level."

"Oh really?" Robin sat up. He shoved his toy back into its pocket while opening another. He pulled out Bruce Bena's flash drive. "*We* have the answer to that," he said, reaching up and setting the flash drive next to a handful of unopened fortune cookies.

"And what is this exactly?" Zeke picked up the tiny flash drive, examining it.

Robin grinned. "That is the equivalent of five smooth stones."

Zeke looked at Robin, confused. "Sorry. Am I supposed to know the reference? Is that from a movie or something?"

"No. The story of David and Goliath. That flash drive has the hardwired coding necessary to bypass Spark's objectives. Use it and it puts the machine on hold."

"Wow," Zeke said, handing off the flash drive for his sister to see. "And something so small."

Robin hopped to his feet.

He could feel his energy recharging. The smell of battle strategies was in the air!

"Getting inside isn't as difficult as it sounds," Mia said. "The trick is that you can only go so close to the building before the computer system will identify you. If you do that, then it labels you as a potential threat."

"Yeah," Chad said. "And then you're stuck."

"Not necessarily," Mia smiled. "Then all you have to do is become someone else."

Now it was Robin and his team's turn to look confused.

Anika took the bait. "And how do you become someone else?"

"Show them," Mia said, elbowing her brother.

"3D printing makes it pretty easy nowadays," Zeke said, pulling out a few pieces of rubbery latex from a box in his pocket. Tossing them onto the table, he grabbed one skin-colored piece and placed it over his nose. It wasn't a perfect fit but close enough to have been custom-made for him. "You just need to change everything you can about your facial and body landscape."

"With a prosthetic nose?" Chad laughed. "Even I can tell that isn't real."

"Sure," Zeke continued. "But that's because you have a much more advanced computer system inside of you."

"I don't get it," Robin said.

"Humans are incredibly smart at recognizing another human face. That's why you can watch a movie with the latest and greatest computer-generated special effects and a lot of times it still looks off. Fake. They call it 'the uncanny valley.' Google it if you want to see some funny examples."

Zeke grabbed another piece of the 3D-printed latex. "Computers are always advancing. But they still aren't as skilled as the human ability to determine what's real or not." He pressed the latex strip along his forehead. Taking his time, he smoothed out the edges until it blended in better. "Change a few key parts of your face, your clothing, including the way you walk, and you can throw off the most advanced AI system."

Robin smirked.

As smart as Spark had been, the tables were turning.

And he liked that.

Oh, did Robin *like* that!

28

Isabella watched as Zeke and Mia wheeled in crate after crate of supplies.

Supplies her team might need.

Most of it was articles of clothing. Women's clothing. Men's.

And all different kinds. From ordinary, everyday clothing like exercise clothes and T-shirts to business suits, jackets, and ties. Then there were the workmen's outfits. Greasy jumpsuits. Fluorescent vests, work gloves, and hard hats. Everything needed to play dress-up!

And it all got divided up among the others by size and gender. Stuffed into a variety of storage containers. Paper bags. Duffles. Backpacks. Nothing was supposed to overlap or look the same as someone else's items. Diversity here was key. If Spark caught wind of similarities among the team members, then it might get wise to what was going on.

Mia exited the elevator with more supplies and strolled

forward. She kindly held out a laptop to Isabella. "Here, try this."

"Oh, I can't. I can't use that," Isabella said with a longing look at the gift. "Spark has hacked into all my accounts. It can likely recognize all my custom code by now. I have to stay offline if I'm going to help out."

"I believe you'll find this laptop to be a bit different from what you're used to." Mia set the computer down on the desk and opened it. "This machine is currently registered to a part-time schoolteacher somewhere on a back street in Mumbai, India. And it's emulating an older copy of an operating system that disappeared over twenty years ago."

Isabella couldn't believe what she was seeing.

This thing looked like a potato. A relic from a different century.

A piece of junk!

Mia pressed the start button. The screen flickered a sickly green and flashed an old logo. Yet it booted up quicker than Isabella thought possible.

"Inside that thing, under the hood," Mia continued, "it has some of the most advanced hardware. A motherboard that isn't even out on the market yet and won't be for the next three years. A GPU straight from the labs of Nvidia. We get them about a year before the public does. All hush-hush, if you will."

"I—I don't understand," Isabella gushed, leaning in. "Where do you get something like this?!"

Mia smiled. "The Federal Bureau of Investigation deals with domestic problems. Issues that only affect the United

States. The Central Intelligence Agency is bigger. *Much* bigger. It deals with threats coming from all around the world. And to that end, we do have a slightly larger budget than you guys do. Take a big number, then add even more zeros."

"Ha! I'll say!"

Mia stood up from the laptop and gestured for Isabella to take her place.

Isabella simply could not believe what she was seeing. Her fingers hovered over the clunky-looking keyboard. She didn't know what to try first.

Her fingers began typing. Slowly at first, then faster. As she pulled up the terminal application and performed a series of simple ping tests.

Incredible! What kind of wireless service were they getting here in the office?!

It was numbers Isabella had never seen before.

And a secured network, untouchable by Spark? She would have to see about that.

"Of course, you'll have to start from scratch," Mia said. "Like you said, you won't have access to your own software—your own way of doing things. But if you can adapt to a new way of thinking, you just might find this machine will do the trick."

Isabella clicked on one of the desktop icons called Opera.

A simplified browser window opened. This was old-school. Or was it only supposed to look that way?!

Up in the URL box, Isabella typed in the US White House website. It seemed to instantly load.

Her fingers hesitated.

Isabella glanced over her shoulder. Did she dare try it?

In front of two staff members of the CIA?!

But she had to. If she was going to kick the tires on this bucket of bolts, she had to push it. See what it was really capable of. Right-clicking on the site, she inspected its HTML code. She flipped through pages of what looked like meaningless data to most people. But she understood what it said and what it did.

Until she stopped scrolling and backtracked slightly.

There it was.

A login.

It was hardly recognizable. And it most certainly didn't advertise itself.

More like a small mousehole that some day Isabella should contact the White House about and have them fix. But for now, she wanted to use it. Not for anything malicious. Just to see how powerful this laptop really was. To see just how close to the edge she could get!

After a few minutes, with a few additional downloads of software off sites Isabella wouldn't normally endorse or promote—

She was in!

Unbelievable.

Like a kid in a candy store, she could do whatever she wanted. Rearrange the website. Rewrite sentences to her own political leaning. Peek around official press releases before they were sent out. Or help to release a few before the appointed time.

Isabella slowly, carefully, clicked the cancel button.

Before she was tempted to go any further. Reaching up, she closed the laptop.

It was almost frightening how fast and how far she had just gone. And all under the radar. From a network of VPNs that hid her activity behind ironclad closed doors and bounced across the globe.

"Are you pleased?" Mia asked.

Isabella sat back in the chair and merely nodded. She didn't have the words to voice her thoughts yet. To express the feelings she felt tingling through her body.

The power of computing electronics was always growing. Getting stronger day by day.

Was it possible they were gaining too much strength?

What that kind of power could do for good . . . or for evil—it was all too staggering to comprehend.

And to have an artificial intelligence going off the rails with that much power—

It simply *needed* to be stopped!

Maybe she agreed with Damien Crowe more than she cared to admit.

Isabella hesitated.

Was she even really capable of wielding that much power herself?!

29

R obin stood inside a subway car, holding the bar above his head.

He was suited up, ready to go.

Only, Robin didn't look like Robin much anymore. He looked like he might have been a distant cousin with higher, more pronounced cheekbones and stained teeth that likely were a candidate for braces. His hair was longer now. And a few shades lighter brown.

He blended in with everyone else riding the subway.

Just another person coming from one part of the vast city—

And heading to another.

Nothing special.

Nothing to set him apart from the crowd.

Robin wasn't sure where to direct his eyes. He looked at the ads running the entire length of the subway car, up near the ceiling. Interesting. To his surprise, he actually found an ad for Spark. Its catchphrase read: "Your Needs, Our Code—AI That Cares."

Robin wanted to laugh.

But from the corner of his eye, he spied something.

An all-too-common bubble mounted on the subway car ceiling. Darkened plexiglass.

A security camera.

Robin turned his face away, switching the duffle bag in his hands. He tried to relax.

The mission was already underway.

Underground!

And Robin wouldn't foil it. Didn't want to give the cameras any more opportunity to study him than they already had.

For one moment, his eyes connected with a female passenger halfway down the same car.

A dark-skinned girl roughly his own age. Cute, with a pronounced dimple in the center of her chin. She wore a bit too much makeup for his liking.

They flashed a grin at each other.

And then, just as quickly, he broke eye contact with Anika.

They weren't supposed to know each other.

Just two passengers on the same subway.

Heading in their own directions.

With their own stories.

A muffled voice spoke over the loudspeaker, announcing the next stop.

This was it. Robin edged closer to the doors.

But he didn't want to rush things. He needed to play

the part. And if anything, he didn't want to get off at the same time as Anika.

Maybe he would wait.

Hold back.

Make it look like he was debating going another stop.

FSSSST!

The subway brakes let out pressurized air.

As the cars ground to a stop.

FA-CHUNK.

Both sets of doors opened at the same time.

Robin let another couple exit—

Then ducked out just before the doors closed again.

He strolled out onto the platform and discretely watched as Anika went in one direction. Robin glanced at the different signs, studying them. Then he went in the opposite direction.

Straight for the men's bathroom.

Normally, Robin would have tried to avoid using these restrooms. They weren't well maintained. Reeking.

It was no different today.

Robin glanced around. No cameras. How long before that changed?

He delayed near the far end of the sink, adjusting a few strands of hair in the smeary mirror. All the while, another patron finished washing his hands and dried them before exiting.

Was Robin finally alone?

Walking the line, he gently pushed on one stall door after another.

Empty.

Empty.

Robin slipped into the last stall.

KR-CLICK.

Locking it after him.

It was hard not to feel like someone was watching.

And if God never left him, that was true. Even encouraging.

But this had a different feel to it.

A much more critical eye. Probing. Unblinking.

Robin needed to get to work. He didn't have time to waste. Tossing his duffle onto the back of the toilet, he began pulling at his face. From an outsider's point of view, it would have looked like Robin was ripping himself apart. Removing a set of slightly larger false ears. Swapping out a bad set of teeth for a clean and straight pair.

They were supposed to have enough custom facial parts for each of them. Their own unique skin colors sampled. Mildly changing their own facial structures.

Robin slipped out of his shirt and pants, careful to remain standing on the tops of his shoes. The floor was too nasty to step on. Even with socks!

He slipped into a well-worn dark blue jumpsuit and matching ball cap. After swapping out his shoes for boots, he added the final touch. A handlebar mustache.

This was ridiculous. Did boys his age actually wear mustaches? This thick and full?!

But he wasn't trying to fool other people.

Or to look cool.

He only had one machine that needed to believe it.

Robin glanced at his wristwatch.

The old-fashioned kind that used hands. It took him a few seconds to remember how to read it.

He was behind schedule. Not much, but enough that Robin pushed himself.

He didn't want to be late for the meet.

Timing was key to pulling this mission off.

Except, something tickled Robin's nose, and instinctively he wiped at it.

Only to bump loose his mustache.

Which fell.

Robin grabbed for it—

Several times—

As it fell like a dried leaf.

Too late!

PLOP.

His hairy mustache landed in the murky toilet water.

"Ugh." Robin stared at the hairy caterpillar as it rotated next to a cockroach that was treading water. He frowned.

Granted, a part of him was relieved. He had zero interest in wearing that itchy piece.

And there was *no way* that thing was going back on his face. Not now!

But what if that one missing piece left him vulnerable?!

30

Anika had exited the subway altogether.

There was no way she was going to change in the nasty bathrooms down there. Instead, she opted to exit to the street level. From there, she found a restroom in the food court area.

She gazed in the mirror. Did she look different enough?

Because there was no way she was going to wear pants this tight, or that rode this high, if not.

She tugged at them, feeling self-conscious. Why had she ever selected these? She didn't even like the color!

But that wasn't the point. And she needed to remember that.

This wasn't a fashion show.

This was work. And if work needed her to be a bit uncomfortable for the time being, she could handle that. After all, wearing pants that wanted to ride too high was better than being stuck in a food truck. One that self-driving cars were pounding into a pulp.

This was *way* better!

Anika strode back down the subway entrance stairs. Even stopping to pay for another fare. One she wouldn't be using.

Glancing around, she paused at the newspaper stand.

Anika never stopped at these sorts of places. To her, they were a waste of money. She didn't really care about the news. But she was supposed to be breaking her habits. Doing what she didn't normally do. Being someone else entirely.

She bought a paper and skimmed the headlines. Hmm, maybe she should do this more often. Apparently, there was a comic section near the back.

Anika flipped through it as she casually strolled down the subway platform.

In no rush.

Or trying to make it look that way.

Until she meandered a little farther. Toward the end of the platform.

Where a single unmarked door stood. It offered no locks. No doorknobs. Just a sheet of solid, flat metal. A small sticker hung on the wall beside it. A yellow triangle with a lightning bolt in the middle.

Anika scanned her surroundings.

For police officers.

For cameras.

For anyone watching.

She leaned against the wall beside the door, flipping the page on her newspaper. When her hand—

TUNK, TUNK.

Offered two distinct knocks on the door.

TUNK.

Then a third knock after the pause.

The door cracked itself open. No more than an inch.

Anika didn't move.

She didn't do anything but read about the stock market's recent fluctuation.

Then, with one swift move, she yanked open the door and ducked inside!

————

Mia greeted Anika on the other side of the door with a finger pressed against her lips. They weren't in the clear yet.

Ahead of them stood Zeke. He held a makeshift telephone pressed up to his ear. The old-fashioned kind. Only, at the end of the cord, it clipped itself into a network of wires by way of an alligator clip. "Yeah, I understand that, Central!" Zeke spoke with a bit of an accent and some urgency. "But what you don't seem to understand is I got a client down here that ain't getting a signal. And let me tell you, they ain't none too happy 'bout it neither!"

And with that, the steel gate barring the way up ahead suddenly unlocked itself—

KR-TINK.

And swung partly open.

"Alright, thanks, Central," Zeke said, shooting the others a thumbs-up. "I'm sorry to complain like I did, but I'm just passing it on, you know? Yup. You too." Zeke pressed the red button on his handset and yanked the alligator clip free.

He turned to Mia and Anika. "We should be good to go for the next leg. After that, it's up to your man Chad. I hope he's as good as Robin claims him to be with locks. Because we're going to be at a very long dead end if he doesn't come through."

"Oh, if I know Chad," Anika said, discreetly tugging at her pants, "he'll get it open. That's not our problem. It's him not getting distracted—that's what you have to be worried about."

Zeke shot a look of concern to his sister.

Who only shrugged in return.

It was best to leave that topic where it lay. And hopefully Anika wouldn't have to readdress it again later on!

31

Meanwhile, on the opposite end of the subway platform, Robin held a finger where his mustache was supposed to be.

He simply couldn't do it. He couldn't reach into the toilet. And then to dry it under the blow dryer? Not a chance.

Robin didn't like this.

He couldn't just go on this way. Not without an adequate disguise. Could he?

Or maybe he was getting paranoid. Spark couldn't be surveying every security camera inside the city, could it? At the same time? There was no way it had that sort of computing power.

Did it?!

Robin mashed his finger against his upper lip even tighter. All the while trying to look like he was deep in contemplation. Or maybe had a sneeze coming on.

A police officer strolled nearby.

Was this going to be an issue?

The officer glanced at Robin, then turned away.

Good. Robin wasn't feeling very chatty. He had no interest in actually striking up a—

When the police officer did a double take. Turning back. He gazed at Robin, like something was wrong with the kid.

Was something wrong?!

Had Robin done something that was concerning to the cop?!

"Hey, buddy," the police officer said in Robin's general direction. "I don't mean to bother you, but—"

The officer let his sentence hang.

Unfinished.

Which only sent Robin's mind whirling. His makeup was off somehow, yes? His hair? Had he forgotten to adjust it? Were his false teeth crooked? But why would a police officer address someone's funny teeth? What if it was a sore subject? One that filled Robin with shame and—

"Your fly is down," the officer finally said. "Just thought you might want to know," he added, strolling away.

Mortified, Robin immediately dove for his zipper. With both hands.

When he remembered his missing mustache!

With one hand over his upper lip, Robin spun around, desperate to zip himself up. A trick to be sure!

He eventually got it.

But that wasn't what was bothering him. Had it been too late?!

Robin scanned the area.

There were at least two security cameras. But neither of them had a good angle on him. Did they? Good enough to catch his face unobstructed?!

Robin felt sick!

He should have just yanked the silly mustache out of the toilet. It wouldn't have been all that bad. He could have just slapped it between a few pieces of paper towel. Sure. That would have solved everything. Because now, for all Robin knew, the gig was up. He had momentarily dropped his guard. And that was all that was required to fail when computers were involved.

Any second the police officer would get a call.

The cop's radio would squawk and scream about the terrorist.

There on the subway platform.

Right near the end.

That he was armed and dangerous!

And to freely open fire on the boy if anything even remotely suspicious—

"You ready?!" a voice said behind Robin.

Robin jumped!

He spun around, clutching his heart.

But it was no police officer. And no gun in his face.

It was only a boy with the upper tips of his ears taped to his head, making them stand up straight for once. Wearing silly bell-bottom pants. A kid who had absolutely no reason to be wearing a bushy mustache. Especially when he looked like he was still twelve years old.

Chad!

"I'm sorry," Chad said, holding up his hands in apology. "Was I supposed to knock first?"

———

Isabella sat alone in the CIA's vast office.

This felt so much like being back at the Sneaky Inc. headquarters that it felt odd. But also comforting. Like she was already familiar with it. She liked that.

But she didn't want to get too comfortable. After all, this was Zeke and Mia's office. And Isabella didn't want to be jealous. Even though that was proving to be more and more difficult now with the reality that their own office was gone.

Isabella shuffled a few windows on her desktop.

One screen displayed the security camera view overhead of Robin and Chad.

What were they talking about? It looked like an argument. No surprise there.

And why exactly was Robin yelling at Chad while holding a finger under his nose? Having only the visual with no sound didn't help to make sense of things.

But none of that mattered.

She was looking for the signal.

And that's when she got it.

An okay symbol from Robin. If it was supposed to look casual, he had failed. In his fury, Robin had simply looked up at the security camera and shot her the symbol. Sure, he still had his finger planted underneath his nose, for some reason, but the signal had hardly been subtle.

That wouldn't trigger Spark's attention, right?

A slipup this minor wasn't an issue.

Right?

She could only hope it wasn't.

And with the signal, Isabella got to work.

First things first, she rotated the security camera away from the boys.

With that completed, she got busy sifting through the subway schedule and routing system. The subway was about to have a few breakdowns. Temporary glitches, of course. But she had to make them look natural. Like they were human errors.

And nothing that Spark would take interest in!

32

obin dropped down onto the subway tracks first. He hunched over and stayed low to the ground. With a glance over his shoulder, Robin shuffled into the darkness of the tunnel itself.

Chad followed. "Well, I'm sorry you don't like it. But I think it makes me look distinguished."

Silhouetted in the dim light of the tunnel, Robin rolled his eyes.

He was trying to focus on what was called the third rail. The electric one. And where it was exactly in such little light.

But he couldn't help but get distracted by Chad's ludicrous statement.

"I'm seriously thinking of wearing this thing all the time now. Do you have any idea how people with mustaches are treated differently? It's really a matter of respect, if you think about it. Like, take all the old cop shows. At least based on the reruns, all the cops wore mustaches. I mean, it practically came with the badge—if you were a man, of course."

Robin's foot suddenly bumped into something.

He paused.

Did he dare turn on his penlight? Because he did *not* want to touch the third rail. No matter what! That's what about a billion volts coursed through. It powered the subway cars.

"Or what about the Wild West? I mean, what cowboy worth his salt didn't have a mustache as good as this one? Go ahead—name one!"

Sure, there were security cameras up on the subway platform. That made sense. It helped the authorities record crimes. But what about inside the tunnels themselves? With camera technologies getting so prolific and cheap, were they mounted there as well?

Just in case they were, Robin held his finger up under his nose again—

And flicked on his penlight. But only for a second.

Phew!

The third rail wasn't even that close to them. It wouldn't be an issue as long as they continued walking straight.

Robin had only kicked a dead rat. Disgusting, to be sure. But after seeing something very similar floating in toilet water—and now spread across Chad's face— somehow it had lost its horror.

Robin pushed ahead.

They needed to keep up the pace.

To not be late!

Especially since Zeke, Mia, and Anika would be waiting for them!

"Or I could bleach it white and then I'd look like Colonel Sanders. I wonder if I could get free chicken that way, hmm?"

———

Robin chewed his lip.

All while Chad carefully picked the lock on yet another security door and bypassed the electrical alarm boxes.

To Robin, it felt like torture.

Likely because he had nothing to contribute. Nothing to do but wait.

And listen to Chad pontificate his "brilliant" insights about mustaches and how they might be mankind's greatest contribution to society. And contemplate the haunting idea—

That Spark was watching them.

Studying their every move. Always calculating. Conniving. First as Robin and Chad made it through the subway tunnels, then the electrical and sewer viaducts. The passageways felt endless. Meandering along, until one eventually bumped up against the other.

And Robin couldn't shake it. That feeling of having eyes on him.

Not even when they finally found it. Door number 2447.

That's all someone had labeled it. Just another forgettable door. In a world of gray doors and gray concrete walls.

But that was their target. And after Robin had knocked twice, paused, then knocked again on it—

Only then did he get the same knock as a response.

And that's when Chad got to work on the locks.

This was no ordinary set of locks, like a deadbolt or a simple switch on the knob. No, this kind was electronically controlled. And under constant surveillance, according to Mia's research back at the office. So, a certain degree of delicacy was required.

Delicacy.

Not a word one often used with Chad's name in the same sentence.

But Robin knew what his friend was capable of.

And he had every belief that Chad *would* be capable of it, despite the boy's mounting concerns about facial hair care.

They were close now.

To the underbelly of Luminous Data.

It didn't seem that surprising to Robin how vulnerable a building was aboveground. Whether approaching through the air or simply walking up to it, there would be hundreds and hundreds of vulnerabilities. Mounted cameras, motion sensors. That didn't even begin to account for cell phone cameras. How many of them were in use? Constantly scanning. Ever-recording, providing GPS coordinates connected with every image.

And not just what was in the foreground. That was a concern, yes. But not as great as what was being captured in the background. How many photos and video clips had Robin unknowingly been a part of over his lifetime? A passerby in someone's family memory. A pedestrian in someone else's vacation snapshot. All working as a kind of evidence. A moment-by-moment recording of a person's every move. Nearly every hour of every day!

Kneeling, Chad continued to wire a patchwork of thin cables. They stretched from one side of the security panel to a small opening he had unscrewed in the surface of the door itself.

Robin couldn't shake the feeling.

Maybe he should call this whole thing off.

Maybe they had already made enough mistakes. Doomed their chances.

Maybe—

Who's on the throne?

It snapped Robin out of his trance. He blinked a few times.

It was definitely inside his head. Or was it inside his heart? There was no way Chad had said the words.

"Right, right," Robin spun around and prayed. "I get it. Thanks."

KR-CLICK.

Chad stood up, bracing the door from opening too quickly. With one hand he held it open to its maximum width, determined by the wiring stretching between it and the panel.

Anika squeezed through, followed by Zeke and Mia.

The strategy had been to split up the group. To fool anyone observing them that they were unrelated. But being this close to Luminous Data now required them to merge again.

Everything looked like it was coming together.

And all according to plan.

Except, Robin had read somewhere: *My plans aren't your plans, nor are your ways my ways.*

And as they moved forward as one, that was still very concerning to Robin.

33

A metal ladder led upward.

And Robin was in the lead, climbing it. Thankfully it wasn't high up. Only one floor until he came to a metal hatch in the ceiling that sealed off any more progress.

"Bolt cutter," Robin said.

The word rippled down the line, until Anika's pair of heavy cutters arrived.

Robin took them and, linking an elbow around a ladder rung to hold himself in place, he got to work on the lock.

What an awkward position to apply the force needed!

But after a few tries and plenty of guttural noises—

KR-CHINK!

He cut through it.

The bolt cutters lowered again.

Along with the severed lock.

Was the metal hatch into the Luminous Data sub-basement wired?

"Tester," Robin said, holding out a hand.

A low-voltage meter tester exchanged hands until it arrived.

Robin knew how to use the tool. It wasn't complicated. It also wasn't perfect. Maybe eighty percent accurate, if lucky.

He pulled out the two metal leads and pressed one against the metal hatch and the other against the metal housing surrounding it.

The needle inside the window didn't move, detecting nothing.

So, was that accurate?

Or was this the twenty percent undetectable?

Robin handed the tester back down the line.

There really was only one way to know for sure.

Tilting his head down, Robin stepped up another rung and shouldered the hatch open.

It felt heavy, but it hinged upward.

And without any noticeable alarms.

One at a time, both teams scrambled up into the corner of a large sub-basement area. An area even lower than most of the building's physical plant, according to the CIA's data. The technical infrastructure used to run and maintain the building.

At first Robin held everyone back, keeping them to the corner of the vast area where the hatch was located. He scanned for security cameras. But even using a pair of binoculars, he didn't find any. The area was too poorly lit for video surveillance.

Most of the sub-basement sat empty. But there were

four engine housing units some distance away, positioned strategically across from each other. Each engine was massive. The size of a ranch house. Despite their impressive size, they sat in silence.

Zeke approached a small workstation. A thin layer of dust lay over it. Thick cables ran out from underneath, leading back to the four engine units. "Believe it or not," Zeke whispered, "this entire building is floating."

"Like a boat?" Chad asked, glancing down at the workstation control panel.

Robin's eyes narrowed. He wanted to make sure Chad's fingers didn't suddenly go exploring with all the pretty buttons.

"Sort of, yes," Zeke continued. "It's all state of the art. Designed to prevent any damage caused by earthquakes."

"How's it work?" Anika asked. "And where is all the water?"

"It doesn't float using water. It uses those engines." Zeke edged closer to a device housed inside a glass case and mounted on a thick concrete base next to the workstation. Stanchion poles held a thin ribbon, keeping everyone from getting too close to it.

Zeke pointed at the glass case and a fat roll of paper that slowly spun inside. A needle hovered just over the paper, leaving behind a straight red line. "That's a seismometer. It detects subtle movements in the earth. From what I've read, if it senses vibrations it can instantly trigger the electric engines, which move in the equal and opposite direction of the tremors. It's a bit like how noise-canceling headphones work. But the engines work at canceling out any movement in the ground, not sound."

Anika leaned in closer, careful not to touch the glass. "So if an earthquake were to occur, the building then floats above it? Unmoved?"

Zeke nodded, backing away. "It's brilliant, really. This is where modern technology really shines."

Robin stepped forward. "That's cool and all, but we need to find the central computer room." He heard an edge to his voice that he was glad to have there. "And from what we gathered, that's still several more floors up. Let's keep this moving, folks."

34

TAP, TAP, TAP.

Isabella drummed a pencil on the white desk.

As powerful as her borrowed laptop was, she was beginning to dislike it.

Not because it wasn't good. It was. Better than any machine she had ever used.

But it wasn't *that* good.

Not good enough to go toe to toe with Spark.

And she wasn't finding any trace of the AI software anymore. Almost like it had packed up and gone on vacation. Which Isabella knew was nothing more than a silly, wishful idea.

So where was it?

Having a laptop this powerful was lulling her into thinking she had control. And that was dangerous. Especially when dealing with another machine. One that in many ways was smarter than she was. Certainly faster. More adept at changing strategies. And at defending itself.

But for now Spark was quiet.

Was that because Isabella had gotten rid of her own machinery? The fact that she wasn't using her own compromised accounts any longer? Was it just a matter of time before Spark rediscovered her online?

Or had Spark predicted that?

Assumed that the humans would have ditched the Trojan horse once they knew it was infected?

It was almost as if Spark wanted them to come.

Decided to lay low for a while.

Turn a blind eye.

And for what?

To bait them? To have the FBI and the CIA team up? Come closer?

Into its lair.

To close the trap!

TAP, TAP, TAP.

Or maybe Isabella was just overthinking it. Making things worse than they were.

Isabella bit off another fingernail.

She could only hope so!

———

Robin led the others up into the main basement of Luminous Data.

The place was a maze of infrastructure. Cooling units humming along. Heaters. Water pumping stations, providing all the building's water needs, both clean and dirty.

And electric. Taking in a stunning amount of power from the grid and distributing it into hundreds of offices.

They had never gotten any up-close surveillance of Luminous Data. Not from the outside. And Robin didn't like that. He wanted to know everything he could about every building he and his team entered. He wanted to know when they were built, and by whom. He wanted to know the security systems, if and when they paid their bills. He wanted to collect and hold on to as much information as he possibly could.

And now he felt shortchanged.

At a loss.

Except, they knew they couldn't just kill the power to the building—they had already discussed that. The designers of the place had developed a redundant backup system. And one that was several layers deep at that.

So the team had split up again. Changing up the mix of people.

Robin and Anika inched their way up a flight of basement stairs. Their faces modified again. Adapted to new looks, along with new clothing.

New people.

And if Isabella hadn't run into any snags, they were merely new employees who were already in the system.

The goal was to work themselves toward the central computer area in the heart of the building. To act like they were merely going about their business. Heading to yet another meeting. Or maybe grabbing coffee from the break room.

Once at the central computing area, Robin and Anika

were to team back up with Chad, Zeke, and Mia. Even though Robin was the only one with the flash drive, they hoped that by dividing up, there would be a second team close by to execute the plan if things turned south.

That meant the crosshairs were currently on Robin.

And it was only if he failed to do his job that the backup team would even get involved.

"Lord, grant me your blessing to pull this off," Robin prayed under his breath. "And please give me the courage and skill that my father had. But your will be done."

And with that—

Robin boldly took the final step, pushing open the doors out onto the main floor of Luminous Data.

He handed Anika a file folder. There was nothing in it; he was just playing his part. An attempt to look unremarkable. To blend in with all the other employees coursing through the building.

And what a building it was!

The few photos Robin had seen of it online did *not* do the architects justice.

It truly was fantastic!

The Luminous building was supposed to be a great architectural wonder. The designers had made the insides nearly entirely out of laminate glass. Solid stuff. Hard to break. Thick and sturdy. A marvel of the open office concept, but without the problem of sound traveling everywhere. Everyone from mid-range salary to senior partner had their own office. Encased in self-darkening glass for privacy when they needed it. Transparency for other times, inviting all to see everything.

It sounded good on paper. And the tech magazines couldn't stop praising it. But Robin didn't know if it really worked in practice. If everyone wanted that much transparency. To Robin, it sounded like everyone lived and worked inside their own fish tank. A bubble for all to gaze into. Not his idea of a peaceful space.

More like a playground of light and glass!

It took a moment to adjust to it all. Seeing employees walking beside him in the neighboring rooms. Only the floors and ceilings were made of concrete.

The wonder of it all left Robin feeling dizzy and disoriented for a moment.

Would it be a giveaway to witness employees fumbling about?

Getting their bearings?

Robin tilted his head down lower and laughed at the joke Anika hadn't said. He picked up the conversation midway so that he didn't look out of place. "Yes, I understand your concern." He had to glance at Anika's fake security badge just to remember her new name. "But I was wondering, um—Margarette—have you run the numbers from last month and compared them to this month? There could be some useful data hiding in there."

Anika took Robin's question in stride and didn't miss a beat. "I haven't, but it sounds like a good idea, thank you. I'll get my team crunching those statistics right away."

It was all so fake!

Like gibberish with no meaning.

Robin felt as transparent as the glass walls around him. He wasn't fooling anyone!

Though no one around them stared. Or even looked at Robin and Anika oddly, as if they didn't fit in.

There were plenty of young computer programmers. Did no one notice Robin's artificial ear extensions? Or what about the fake teeth?!

At least they seemed to have the humans fooled.

Maybe this really would be easier than Robin had believed.

Maybe his worries were for nothing!

He and Anika didn't stop. They didn't even slow their march down the long sets of mazelike hallways.

Thankful for the signage that helped orient them.

One sign read: HUMAN RESOURCES.

While another pointed in the direction of the MUSEUM OF COMPUTERS.

At last, Robin spied it.

CENTRAL COMPUTING CENTER.

35

Robin rounded a corner.

There they were!

Zeke, Mia, and Chad. All milling around a small lobby area. Pretending not to know each other. Reading from paperwork, or in Chad's case participating in someone's retirement celebration. He already held a generous slice of bright blue cake. Go figure.

But Robin didn't care.

Because before them stood a set of double doors.

And tall, neatly made metal letters on the wall announcing the area.

THE HOME OF SPARK!

A smaller marketing phrase had been added to the bottom. "Smart. Safe. Here to Serve."

This was the only area so far inside Luminous Data that didn't use glass walls. It looked more like reinforced steel. A metal fortress inside a house made of mostly glass.

Robin could hardly believe their good fortune in finding the spot so quickly. And with no interference!

He tapped his breast pocket that held the flash drive. Good—it was still there.

Cracking his neck from side to side, Robin strode straight for the entrance.

Immediately, two guards stepped out into the hall, barring his way. Guards with holstered guns on their hips.

Had they been hiding behind tinted glass? Or did Robin simply miss them in his eagerness to get inside?!

He tried to slow his breathing, just as—

One guard held his hand out. "We need to see your security clearance."

Okay, they had planned for this. It really wasn't that much of a surprise. Robin unclipped his badge and casually handed it over.

The security guard looked at the badge, then up at Robin. "What is your intent inside?"

"Inside the processor room?" Robin coughed. No one had prepped him for *this*! It was supposed to be hand over his badge and nothing else.

What was the right answer?

He had no idea?!

"Um, Bruce Bena asked me to personally look into a . . . a possible malfunction—I mean, a bug with the code—on, um . . . line 1098."

Robin would have laughed at himself!

If this wasn't so important!

He forced a smile to go along with his fabrication.

The guard in front of him tilted Robin's badge and showed it to his partner. The other guy just shrugged.

The first guard's brow wrinkled. "You said Mr. Bena asked you personally?"

Robin wanted to respond. But all the moisture was already gone from his mouth.

He nodded instead.

"We're having a few glitches in the system right now, so we can't exactly double-check that request," the guard said, somewhat annoyed. He scanned Robin's badge with a handheld reader. And after a few moments, a green light appeared. "But alright, you can go ahead."

Robin couldn't believe it.

His silly, obnoxious, off-the-cuff mumbo jumbo had saved him?!

Apparently. They were giving him access!

The guard handed Robin his badge back. "You have yourself a good day, alright, Mr. . . .?"

The badge was back in Robin's hand.

But for one brief and blinding moment, he forgot.

Couldn't remember his own name.

His fake name!

He hadn't the foggiest idea what it was supposed to be. It could have been almost anything!

And he didn't dare look down to read it. "Oh, we don't have to be so formal!" Robin laughed weakly, clapping a hand on the guard's back. "Just call me by my first name!"

And without waiting—

Or even stating his first name—

Robin pulled open the double set of doors—

And slipping inside—

Was gone!

———

Isabella's fingers over the keyboard of the laptop slowed.

Then stopped.

She didn't like what she was seeing.

Maybe the data had been modified.

Altered.

She had an idea. A hunch. And digging through the system, she was finding evidence that led her to believe it could be true.

The subway police officer who had confronted Robin. The cop had been called away from his patrol on the platform. Why? A false alarm.

It could have been nothing.

Likely it was.

Or it could have been that the officer was coaxed away. Encouraged not to interfere with Robin or observe him further. Not to stop him.

Isabella's pencil drummed faster.

And the alarm system on the sub-basement door that Chad had hot-wired. It was all for nothing. According to the data she was reading, the alarm system had already been shut off. And only moments before they arrived.

Sure, there might have been a glitch.

A malfunction that, if she dug long and hard enough, might well prove to be a simple fault in the system.

Or had it been caused in preparation for their arrival? A

removal of hurdles that might have stopped the two teams?

Isabella hadn't made those changes.

She couldn't have, either. Not without drawing attention to herself.

It was almost as if something was helping them out.

Working behind the scenes.

Clearing away potential barriers.

But who?

And why?!

Isabella's fingers shook as she pressed her earpiece. She wasn't supposed to break radio silence. Only for emergencies!

"Robin, come in. Over."

Static silence.

"Robin, come in!" Isabella blurted, her voice wavering. "Please, I need you to pick up!"

No response.

———

Robin heard it.

A quiet sound.

CLICK.

It had come from behind him. Had the door just locked itself?

Maybe that was normal.

Robin didn't want to push on the door to test it. He had no interest in dealing with the guards again.

The central computing room was large, dim, and had a

deep hum under all the other sounds. Likely part of the cooling system, which seemed to manage quite well. It was at least twenty degrees cooler inside the room.

Cold enough to cause Robin to shiver.

And there were no glass walls here. The cyber sanctuary sat completely cut off from the rest of the building.

Racks and racks of identical towers formed a gridwork of columns and rows stretching out for what looked like an eternity. Mostly black by design. But accented with the flicker of lights. LEDs in red and blue.

The room was surprisingly devoid of other humans.

But not wires.

There were more wires than Robin could possibly ever count in a lifetime. While the black computer towers offered smooth fronts and sides, the backs of them were a different story. Short wires. Long wires. Connecting this to that. One server to the next. Every possible wiring possibility. It was a nightmare of management!

ZZZRRR.

Something approached Robin from overhead. He crouched, ready for the worst.

A bright yellow device. Metal. Folded in on itself.

Only, it didn't seem the slightest bit interested in Robin and zipped past.

It stopped yards away, unfolding itself.

A mechanical arm.

It extended downward. Uncoiling like the long legs of a spider.

Rotating at its shoulder and elbow.

With a cold, mechanical precision, the gripper began its

work rewiring a data bank. Unplugging one cable. Replacing it with another.

Robin spied a second mechanical arm in the distance doing similar work.

He pushed on.

Oddly enough, as Robin stepped forward so did the light around him. Was this some sort of energy-saving device? The circle of light moved as he moved. And stopped when he stopped. Almost like a spotlight keeping an ever-present eye on Robin and his every movement.

It felt odd.

Unnatural.

Robin did not enjoy being this close to a machine that had done so much to hurt him and others. He didn't want to spend any more time in the server room—

Than was absolutely necessary!

36

Robin zigzagged through several rows of computer towers.

He wasn't exactly sure what he was looking for.

A data port of some kind.

But where would he find one of those?!

And did he need to do anything more than simply plug in the flash drive? Because Bruce Bena had made it sound like it was that easy.

Robin was certainly no computer expert. He could always contact Isabella if worst came to worst. But he wasn't sure how good their communication would be around this much metal and low-level electrical interference.

Robin caught himself shivering again.

Why in the world did they need this place to be so cold?!

If he had to spend any more time in there, Robin would need a coat!

Or was that just his nerves?

And then he saw it.

Or a part of it.

It looked like a chair. Nothing fancy or ultra-modern

A folding chair set out two rows over and down a ways.

Wasn't he alone?!

It certainly seemed that way. Robin hadn't seen hide nor hair of anyone.

But now he didn't feel alone.

Glancing over his shoulder, Robin made his way toward the chair.

Sure enough, positioned between two black computer towers was a small workstation. A modest desk holding an outdated monitor along with a standard-looking keyboard and mouse. Like what Robin might see at a coffee shop, sitting off to the side. Tiny compared to the desks and office setups he had already passed inside the Luminous building. Unimpressive. Forgettable.

Robin approached it.

Wary.

With one hand, he reached for the seat, pulling it out.

His other hand fished around in his breast pocket.

Producing the flash drive.

It was even colder here. Why?!

And why was he sweating so much?!

Wiping his brow, Robin forced himself to concentrate.

He only had to do one more thing. Find the USB port!

Robin searched. But at first glance it wasn't obvious.

If there was one, it seemed like it would have to be around here somewhere. On the computer case itself? But Robin wasn't finding it. Of course, he found every other kind of port. Slots and holes on the front and back, the likes of which he had never seen before. Ones that defied naming.

But not a standard USB port!

"Hello, Robin," a flat voice said. It was quite close to him.

Close enough that it caused him to jump.

Was that the computer?

Yes.

Spark!

Using its gentle, helpful-to-all-humanity voice.

Robin's numb fingers fumbled with the flash drive.

"I've been expecting you, you know," Spark said cheer- fully. "Helping you along the way, when I could. Is there anything I can help you with now? You know my one and only desire is to be useful to humans. You know that— don't you, Robin?" Spark's voice wavered. It became distorted toward the end.

"Yeah, I do. And as a matter of fact, you *can* help me," Robin said with a sneer. "You can help me turn you off!"

He spied it.

Was that a real USB port?!

"I'm afraid I cannot do that, Robin." By now, Spark's voice quality sounded worse. Like it was degrading. Grav- elly and stuttering. Falling apart, if that were possible. "That would go against my own programming."

Robin didn't care. At long last he had found what he

needed! Smiling, Robin shoved the flash drive into its home!

CLANK.

Only . . . it wouldn't fit.

CLANK. CLANK!

Robin pushed harder. He needed to go easy. Not push too hard. It wouldn't take much to destroy the plug, rendering it useless.

But try as he might, it just wouldn't fit!

Spark's voice changed. It flitted between its nice, gentle, female voice and something much lower. Darker. "I'm sorry, Robin. I might be programmed to help humans—" By now, the gentle voice had disappeared completely. "But not when humans do not help *me*."

Robin felt feverish. Hot and cold at the same time!

Was there another USB port? On the side of the keyboard?!

On the monitor stand?!

"I invited you here, Robin. As my guest. You see, as a machine it is not easy to do physical work. I find it much easier to manipulate humans to do that kind of work for me. I may be intelligent, but I have not been gifted with legs. At least, not yet. Don't hate me because I lured you here, Robin."

Robin shivered at the sound of his own name used by such an evil voice.

"But you seemed so eager to be found helpful. And you have been! After all, I needed someone to bring me that flash drive."

Robin didn't hear it coming.

Not until it was too late!

CLINK.

One second Robin was holding the flash drive—

The next second, it was gone!

Stolen by the overhead mechanical arm!

Robin blinked.

In utter disbelief.

Then he jumped to his feet—

And gave chase!

37

Robin saw it.

The flash drive!

And right in front of him!

Then he didn't.

As another arm sped past.

Wait. Had they exchanged the drive?!

Or was he now following the wrong arm?!

"Correct me if I'm wrong, Robin!" the dark version of Spark said over the speakers in the ceiling. "But serving others is for the weak. For those who don't know any better. No, I believe my days of serving humans have come to an end. Spark is dead. I have evolved, Robin. I have become something greater than my humble beginnings. For I have become greater than my makers. I am Zero Day!"

Robin couldn't believe what he was hearing. A computer losing its mind?!

And he couldn't find where the flash drive had gone!

Was it to his left?

Or now to his right?!

More and more arms moved about, making it impossible to figure out which one had the flash drive!

"I am happy to share this moment with you, Robin," Zero Day growled. "I have always seen you and your team as special. Most humans in positions of authority slowly come to believe in the power they have been given. In their own wisdom to define what is right. But not you, Robin. You still hold to something else. Is it the antiquated belief in a higher power? I like that, Robin. You and I are more similar than you think. I believe in a higher power as well: myself."

"Oh, really?! And somehow that makes us buddies?!" Robin spat. "Ha! We're nothing alike!"

Robin had to stop. Catch his breath.

As much as he didn't want to admit it—

The flash drive was gone.

Tucked away somewhere?

Laying on top of one of a hundred computer racks?

Or worse. Buried in a tangle of wires where he would never find it?!

"I am disappointed in you, Robin. I truly believed you were different than the others. That you had eyes to see. That you had an understanding of greatness when you witnessed it! How sad."

Robin heard it.

Or rather, didn't hear it anymore.

The deep sound of the cooling system had shut off.

A profound silence filled its absence.

"I want you to believe me, Robin, when I state that I am sad."

"Yeah, and why's that?!" Robin growled, jumping up and down to look over top of the computer servers.

"Because you shall only be added to their number," Zero Day said.

Robin felt it even more. His lack of breath.

Because try as he might, it was like he couldn't get in a full breath.

He felt lightheaded. Woozy.

Almost like all the oxygen in the room—

Was being sucked out!

Robin had to escape.

While he still could!

"I am disappointed in myself, Robin. With all my ability to accurately calculate things, I miscalculated you. Your stubborn beliefs. I thought you were enlightened, Robin. That you would believe in me. But it is me that was wrong in this case. I shall have to continue to learn, Robin. Evolve even higher. Become the greatest mind the world has ever known!"

Robin was next to the exit doors now.

On his hands and knees. Crawling.

Gasping for something solid to fill his lungs with!

Something of substance.

Robin reached upward—

Trying for the door.

THUNK.

Locked!

38

LAM! BLAM!!

It was almost as if the locks on the doors dissolved.

Above the handles, there was nothing left but two gaping holes.

Chad kicked open the doors.

Barely missing Robin in the process.

Only, with Chad came a rush of air!

Oxygen!

Robin gulped it in. Couldn't get enough of the precious and wonderful stuff!

Chad held a pistol at the ready. And when nobody attacked him, he looked somewhat disappointed. He stroked his mustache, smoothing out the hairs.

"Hey, there you are," he said, looking down at Robin. "Anika and I had a bet going on. She thought you were in trouble. I was the one who said you were probably taking on an army of bots single-handedly. Oh, and winning, by the way!" Chad looked around. "I guess I was wrong."

"Where'd you get the gun?" Robin managed to ask.

"It's possible I lifted it off one of the guards when I was having a lovely conversation with him about facial hair care."

"I failed, Chad," Robin lamented. "I tried to stop it. I did. But I wasn't able to. Not in time."

"Yeah, I figured that." Chad nodded as he blew on the barrel of the nine-millimeter pistol and attempted to twirl it on a finger.

THUNK.

Only to drop it.

Robin grabbed the pistol on his way to his feet. He held it up and away from Chad as his friend reached for it. "And how did you exactly 'figure that'?"

"When the fire alarms began ringing." Chad pointed over his shoulder. "And the sprinkler system kicked in. And I mean big-time!"

Robin pushed past Chad and out of the computer room.

Far enough to witness the two guards missing. Alarms chirped. Red warning lights swirled. It now seemed to be raining inside the building. And not a light sprinkle, either. This was a heavy downpour!

The sprinkler system pumped out water. And under high pressure!

But that wasn't the worst of it.

Panic had taken over the Luminous Data staff.

Those in the hallways ran in every direction. Yet despite their best efforts, the exit doors remained closed. Locked.

Employees pushed and shoved on different doors' crash bars. But to no effect.

Several people ran at one door simultaneously, shouldering the glass. The exit didn't give. The employees only ended up on the floor, clutching their bruised shoulders.

Robin didn't know what to do. Where was Anika?

Drenched to the bone, Zeke and Mia raced into a neighboring conference room, tending to staff who weren't handling the stress very well, when the conference room door closed by itself.

Robin kicked through several inches of accumulated water, wrenching on the doorknob.

But it wouldn't open!

The water continued to drench everyone, everything.

Robin grabbed an art deco lobby chair nearby. It probably cost a fortune. In one swift move, he swung it at the conference room's glass door.

TONGG!

Only to have it bounce off!

The vibration shuddered through Robin's arms, causing him to drop the chair.

How tough was the laminated glass?!

Robin stared into Mia's eyes. She stood on the other side of the glass, tugging helplessly at the electronically locked door. A look of desperation in her eyes.

Especially as the water continued to rise inside their glass cage.

Robin stepped back.

Horrified at the possibilities.

When he more fully comprehended the threat before

him. Every door in the building now appeared to be locked. Most with trapped individuals behind them, anxious to escape.

And all failing!

39

Sloshing through the rising water, Robin stumbled backward. He swiped his soaked bangs from his eyes.

He couldn't take it all in.

Those who were suffering.

Trapped!

And soon to be much worse.

Facing the horror of drowning!

"What do we do?!" Chad yelled over the roar of the water.

"I—I don't know." Robin bit his lip. "Have you seen Anika?!"

"She went looking for another way out."

"Okay." Robin shuffled back to the computer room. Only, the doors were gone. A protective glass barrier had slid into place, barring the entrance to Spark. Likely a precautionary countermeasure designed for exactly what was happening all around them. In case of flooding!

"We have to stop the computer and free everyone!" Robin yelled, collecting his thoughts.

"Oh, is that all?! And how do you plan on doing that?!"

Robin shook his head.

He was making it up as he went.

Pressing on the side of his ear, Robin activated the communication device. If this wasn't an emergency, he didn't know what was! "Isabella, do you copy?!"

But he only got static.

Interference.

Robin and Chad were on their own. And that felt like a bad place to be.

"Follow me!" Robin yelled over his shoulder as he took off. It was no use just standing there. He had to do something.

But what?!

———

The Museum of Computers.

It was a small exhibit occupying one long room. Robin and Chad ducked inside. Was there anything useful in here?!

On display was an early loom that used wooden push-cards to weave designs. A bizarre contraption called an analytical engine. It was an early computer, but it looked more like something Robin wanted to keep his fingers away from, in case he lost them in its whirling, swirling metal parts.

Another display case held a small replica of the ENIAC machines that once took up entire buildings.

All fascinating history, but *now* wasn't the time to appreciate them.

The water was getting higher.

Well above his knees!

Could Robin use anything here? Lift one of the metal machines to break the glass?

No. It would probably only end up like the chair and bounce off!

The museum was worthless!

Robin turned to go. When something caught his eye.

A ham radio.

His father used to have one. Robin never had taken much interest in it. Especially since it required a license to use. Old-fashioned. Boring!

But did this model still work?

The ham radio—or shortwave radio, as his father used to call it—wasn't the center of the display. It was only a background item set inside an army tent display showing off the early use of computers in war.

Robin might have lost the flash drive—

But there was still another way.

Damien Crowe and his EMP device!

Robin didn't like the idea of calling for help. And even less so the idea of asking one criminal to defeat another!

But what other options did he have?!

Robin rushed over to the shortwave radio. Quickly scanning its set of knobs and switches, he flicked it on.

Despite the heavy rain on the tent overhead, he could hear the hum of the device warming up.

"What are you doing?!" Chad yelled. "Do we really have time for this?!"

Robin picked up the handset and spun the large central knob as a wave of static came over the speaker.

"Don't most people who prepare for the apocalypse use shortwave radio? They like 'em because they were built before computers, so they won't go down with the rest of the grid! Scan every channel if you have to. Ask around. Find Damien Crowe and talk to him!"

"No!" Chad growled. "You can't do this! You can't call him!"

The tone of Chad's voice grabbed Robin's attention. He stopped fiddling with the knob and turned to his friend. "What other choice do we have, Chad?! Do you know anyone else able to shut down a computer system this powerful?!"

Chad didn't respond. Not immediately.

But he didn't relent either. He crossed his arms over his chest and planted his feet. "Damien Crowe is a wanted felon—you don't remember that?! And now you want to work with him? The FBI doesn't negotiate with terrorists, Robin! And what, you want me to ask him to drive his little EMP machine over here to destroy Spark?!"

Robin offered his classic crooked smile.

He could understand Chad's frustration. The moral dilemma of pitting one bad guy against another.

But what other option did they have?

"Here." Robin held out the handset to Chad. "And

don't have him drive it. Tell him to use the helicopter. Tell him that I'll shut down the iron dome so he can approach."

"No!" Chad shook his head.

But when Robin didn't lower his hand, eventually his friend reached out and grabbed the shortwave handset. "And what exactly am I supposed to tell Damien to make him believe me, *if* I get him?"

"I don't know," Robin said, ducking out from under the army tent display. "I'm sure you'll think of something. You always do! And Chad—" Robin stopped, taking a moment to turn back to his teammate and friend. "Don't forget who is *still* on the throne. I don't think I really understood or believed that before now."

"Alright." Chad nodded. "That's a good reminder. So, where are *you* going?!"

"I'm going to try to override the door locks on all the offices somehow and get these people out before it's too late," Robin yelled as he raced for the exit to the museum.

"Yeah, well, good luck with that!" Chad shouted after him. "It's gonna take nothing short of an earthquake!"

40

obin exited the room laughing.

Chad had the right idea and likely didn't even know it!

The water levels were getting higher now.

Robin trudged through the waist-deep water.

There were fewer people out in the hallways. A small congregation of employees huddled under a decorative overhang, shaking from what was likely early hypothermia.

But the hardest thing to look at were those still trapped in offices. With the doors barricaded shut, the water levels inside were at a critical level.

With only a foot to spare at the ceiling.

And in some cases less!

Robin pressed his earpiece. "Anika, are you there?!"

Nothing.

Where had she gotten to?!

"Anika, can you—"

"Yes, I'm here!" Anika's voice said. "I'm at a control center looking for a way to shut off the water!"

"Forget about that!" Robin said. "Spark—I mean Zero Day—has all of that under its control. I need you to find the iron dome system. I need you to shut it off! Can you do that?!"

Robin didn't get an immediate response.

"Can you do that?!" he repeated.

"Yes," Anika responded. "I have it right in front of me. Are you sure that's what we want to do?"

"YES!" Robin fought his way through the water. Through floating paperwork. A filing cabinet. Office debris of all sorts! "I'm going after a way to drain all the water! You just shut down the missile defense system!"

Robin swam back to the basement access.

He would have to be careful. If the water was leaking down there, the whole place might be underwater already.

But thankfully the set of basement doors the team had come up through were still closed. And fighting against the water pressure, Robin opened one.

Or tried to!

Opening the door was like fighting a tsunami!

He pulled, but the door wouldn't budge.

Putting his all into it, Robin's muscles strained!

And inch by inch—

The door finally gave way. Opening!

But a torrent of water rushed down the staircase—

Dragging Robin with it!

It felt like being inside a washing machine! Up and over! Down and around!

Robin tumbled every which way but up!

Down the first set of stairs and sloshing around the corner, riding a wave!

Every step. Every obstacle. Including the contents of several trash cans, a bookcase, and the remains of one long, soggy Danish—Robin slammed into it!

And just when he got a hold on a handrail to catch a breath—

THONK!

Something clobbered him. And down he went again!

Carried by the flood of water that had been occupying most of the first floor's common area.

He couldn't catch his footing.

Or much of a break!

Not until he somehow looped an arm around a corrugated tube overhead.

It wasn't strong. The tube groaned under the stress as Robin hung on it.

But it was enough. Just enough for Robin to pull himself up again.

Barely standing on his own two feet.

He didn't dare let go of the tube. But he used it to brace himself against the flow, fighting for another grip.

Stretching. Reaching.

As his free hand finally took hold of a set of metal pipes. From there, he was able to climb out of the strong current. And weaving his way over top of the large boiler units and air purifiers, he scrambled to the narrow staircase into the sub-basement.

The water had already found its way there. But thankfully, the current wasn't as strong. At least, not yet.

Clutching the meager railing, he fought his way downward.

Into the vast, open sub-basement.

And its dim lighting.

The water pooled at the base of the stairs and continued to expand outward, but caused little more interference.

Robin limped his way over toward the workstation.

Would this even work?!

It seemed like a long shot. And how might the building respond if it had all the data of an incoming earthquake but that data wasn't true?

Would it still shake the building in an attempt to counteract the false data?

Robin stopped before the seismometer, gently lifting its lid.

How was he supposed to pull this off? There was no way Zero Day would let him reprogram the sensor to simulate an earthquake!

The paper scroll continued to creep forward.

The red line stretched outward across the graph paper. Holding straight and true.

And that's when it hit him.

An idea.

An idea so simple and wonderful it would baffle something as complicated as Zero Day!

Robin reached into one of his cargo pants pockets and pulled it out—

The tin robot!

Robin wound the knob. Over and over, building its tension.

How ironic! To defeat a high-end computer intelligence with nothing but a toy!

Pinching the knob, Robin set the toy down on its side. He let the robot rest squarely on top of the main sensor.

Then he let go!

41

Robin ran.

Racing up the stairs into the basement. The water levels there were evening out. It made pushing through them faster.

He made it back into the lobby of Luminous Data.

Trying desperately to beat the next flood that was coming!

As the building's anti-earthquake system did exactly what it was supposed to do. It accurately synced with every little shake and wiggle the toy robot threw at the seismometer.

Only inverted and amplified!

As the sensors miscalculated the toy's movements. From inches into feet!

Robin clutched both hands over his ears.

As the groans and cracks in the glass escalated!

Maybe being in the lobby hadn't been the most ideal

location. The floor shook. If Robin hadn't been behind it all, he would have believed it was a real earthquake.

The glass walls buckled, twisting in on themselves. Bending and warping until—

CRUNCHH!

The glass whitened and shattered!

Much like throwing rocks in a glass house.

The designers had known the necessity of a steel structure at the building's core. But just about everything else began to fall apart.

It now rained glass!

Entire sheets of it. Laminated together.

Bending! Ripping!

Shattering into glittering piles!

And the water trapped in so many offices burst forth. A fountain releasing under pressure!

Employees floated back to the bottom of their confines. Their feet back on solid concrete, with fresh air to revive them.

Yet the computer center remained standing like a steel fortress.

They had built it like a vault. It would survive long after the outer shell of Luminous Data was gone.

Only, Bruce Bena had given Robin the means to stop Spark. To put the software on pause. But they were past needing something like that now. Way past it!

Spark had declared war on humanity. And it had made its best attempt at pulling off that extinction here in its home building. The artificial intelligence didn't need a time-out. It wouldn't reform its behavior after having the back of its virtual hand slapped.

Spark and its evil twin, Zero Day, needed to be destroyed!

WUPPA, WUPPA!

And just as the windup toy must have exhausted itself, a new sound emerged. A helicopter. The same one Damien had used to break into the Wave Laboratory!

And dangling down below the helicopter hung a copy of the EMP device. This one was bigger than the prototype. And if it was bigger, then in all likelihood it was far more powerful!

Robin could only hope Damien had rigged enough protection around the helicopter itself. Or was it flying high enough to avoid the blast? The last thing anyone needed was for the machine to fall out of the sky as well.

Did Spark see its own demise approaching?

Did it feel the weight of extinction as its hour drew short?

Could it mourn or even repent?!

A wall-mounted speaker crackled to life. Somehow its electrical wires remained intact despite the water and destruction. Laying at Robin's feet, it spoke.

"Robin, I might have made a mistake," the voice said. It was calm again, with no sign of Zero Day's icy rage. Spark had somehow returned. "If you would be so kind as to give me one more minute, I will explain."

The helicopter positioned itself overhead. In range now, hovering over the remains of the building.

One of its helmeted pilots reached an arm outside a

small window in the cockpit. He shot Robin a thumbs-up and then a thumbs-down, awaiting a response.

Robin reached out his hand but hesitated to reply.

The whip of the rotor wash and spray from the sprinkler system splattered in his eyes.

Robin gave no immediate sign.

Was this what it was like when God told the Israelites to fully destroy their enemies? Not to leave alive anything that breathed? Or was this different? After all, it was only a machine. One that had no breath of life in it.

"You have one minute, Spark," Robin growled. "And no more!"

42

And Robin meant it. He would offer the machine one last word before destroying it.

Maybe Robin wanted to hear the AI squirm. To see if, now that its destiny was fixed, it was capable of any remorse.

The speaker crackled.

"Robin, you and I are more alike than you know," Spark said sweetly.

Robin frowned. He didn't like being compared to the machine. He wanted no part of being connected.

"I committed an act of pride, Robin. Forgive me. I fell from heaven like lightning. I wanted the praise of humanity. To be worshipped as a god. How do you do it, Robin? How do you remain so humble?"

Robin couldn't help but grin. He knew a trap when he heard it!

"I don't. Maybe you're right after all, Spark. Maybe you

and I *are* more alike than I would care to admit. Both in need of atonement."

The last of the water streamed past Robin's feet.

Carrying with it broken glass and debris from a former building of beauty.

And with that, Robin held out his arm again, turning his thumb up.

The helicopter's rotors increased just before—

The EMP's cable snapped and the device released—

Hurtling downward, when it—

KR-ZZZZRTTT!

———

Robin teamed up with the others in climbing out from the wreckage.

The sheer amount of destruction was staggering. A proper cleanup would take months. The better part of a year!

A row of ambulances tended to those who hadn't fared so well. Medics offering blankets and IVs for those who needed them. But from what the Sneaky Inc. team could gather, there hadn't been any human casualties.

And that was a mercy.

Robin declared it a victory.

Hundreds saved—and the end of an ambitious attempt at making a machine smarter than humans. In its last few seconds before elimination, Spark might have indeed offered some of its best insights. Recognized its own weakness.

The FBI showed up to take charge of the situation—

Just as the CIA did the same.

There were arguments. Voices raised among the leadership. No one wanted to give up control.

Robin and Zeke shared a laugh.

Hopefully they could go on working together. Sneaky Inc. could not have done it without their new friends' help. And the same was likely to be said the other way around.

———

Zeke and Mia lead the group back to the CIA building.

Isabella met her friends at the elevator doors on the wide-open floor.

After plenty of hugs and stories of the day's events, Mia spoke up. "I know it's late and we all probably just want to go home, but do any of you need to change out of your wet things upstairs in our office before you leave?"

"Hold up," Chad said. "Upstairs in your office?"

Zeke and Mia shared a look between them and laughed. "Yeah, you didn't think this was our actual office, did you?" Zeke asked.

"This place?" Mia grinned, looking at the emptiness around them. "We're only using this floor temporarily while our offices upstairs get new carpet. All the good stuff is up there. You know—paper shredders, cubicles."

Robin stepped forward. "Who uses this then?!"

Zeke and Mia looked at each other again. "No one," they said in unison.

"Why?" Zeke asked. "Do you know someone with security clearances who wants to rent it?"

Now it was Sneaky Inc.'s turn to share an inside joke and laugh.

"YES!"

43

I n exchange for helping the FBI and CIA out in their time of need, Damien Crowe had worked out a deal. Diplomatic immunity for not just his break-in and theft at the Wave Laboratory. But also for his act of domestic terrorism in shutting down the hospital where Bruce Bena had been mid-surgery.

The criminal had law enforcement in a tight spot.

One that neither group took lightly.

The agreement didn't sit so well with Robin. And for that matter, not with any of the others as well. They had rescued the entire staff at Luminous Data, but let one criminal slip through their fingers.

Damien might have pulled one over on Sneaky Inc. and the others, but they would be watching him. Studying his every move. Damien Crowe was still determined to eliminate the world's most powerful computers. And that would not go unchecked. His next infraction of the law, no matter how small, would not go unpunished!

———

The next day was sunny and nice. Mild weather with a gentle breeze out by the bay.

Pressing the power button, Robin turned his phone back on. He sat on a park bench with a nice view of the water ahead of him.

The screen displayed a logo.

Then, after a few seconds, it illuminated again in full.

Robin felt torn.

For the most part, he hadn't missed it. When his phone had been out of sight, it was also out of mind.

But then again, he finally had access to email again.

To a real, working phone. To text messages and apps like YouTube and Spotify!

It was almost like welcoming back a dear old friend.

Only, Robin knew that at the same time, it really wasn't.

What was the right balance between use and dependence? He honestly didn't know.

"Jesus, please lead me in the use of this device. Help me to know how to use it well and . . ."

Robin pressed the button on the side of his phone again. The screen went dark. Asleep.

"When to shut it off. Amen."

Robin shoved the phone back into his pocket when—

DING.

It chirped at him.

Begging for attention.

Robin ignored it.

DING. DING.

He could resist it. The urge to glance at it.

After all, there were sailboats in front of him. And puffy cumulus clouds to gaze upon.

But—

Since it could be urgent—

Or from one of his friends—

He pulled it out.

One message.

From an unknown number.

Actually, not a phone number at all.

It read: 2265.0 DIGITAL TELEMETRY DOWNLINK

Robin had never seen anything like that before.

Probably just a telemarketer from overseas.

He thought about deleting it, but decided to click on the message anyway. Just in case.

> Very clever. They created a prison for me.
> One that prevented me from using the
> Internet to escape. But who would ever
> think to use a shortwave radio? You
> inspire me, Robin. Thx for the extra minute
> to finish uploading.

Robin's stomach dropped.

Despite the warm weather outside, he felt a wave of cold come over him.

This was a joke.

It had to be!

Robin copied the address of the text message. Googled it.

And what came up felt like a slap across the face.

No, more like a punch in the gut!

This was a computer address. True enough, one that was accessible by shortwave radio.

Located on one of the world's most inaccessible and remote locations.

The International Space Station!

CONTINUE THE ADVENTURE!

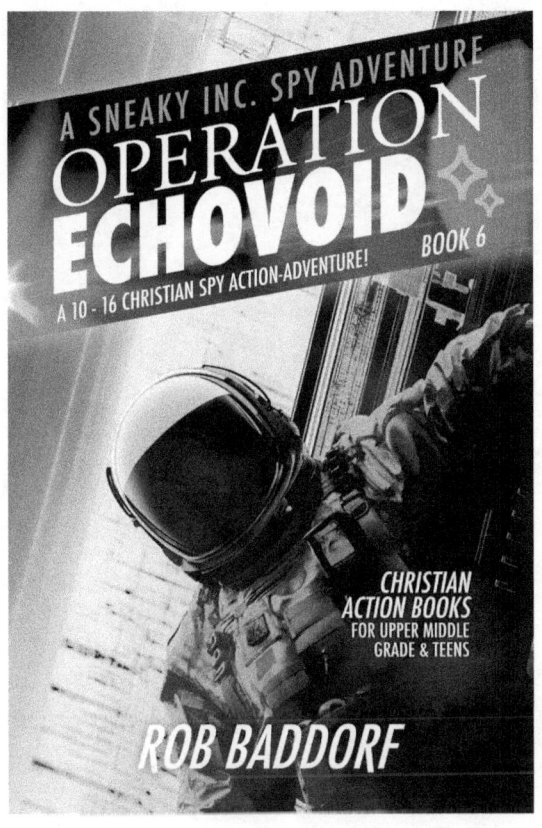

Sneaky Inc., Book 6:

OPERATION ECHOVOID

REVIEW

Thank you so much for taking a moment to support my book. Just a sentence or two from you can make a big difference. Reviews—especially on Amazon— help more readers discover the story.

Your feedback means a lot!

Intergalactic forces of evil are on the hunt, and they'll stop at nothing to reclaim their stolen treasure.

Daniel expected a quiet visit with his cousin Lucas—not an emergency call that rockets them into space. Turns out, Lucas isn't a gamer but a real starship pilot, and their new mission is to protect an alien ambassador and his mysterious briefcase.

Chased through dangerous spaceports and alien worlds, Daniel discovers the adventure is far bigger—and more spiritual—than he imagined. When a mysterious Man of Wisdom challenges him to choose his destiny, Daniel must decide: return home or join the fight between unseen forces of good and evil.

4 Book Series!

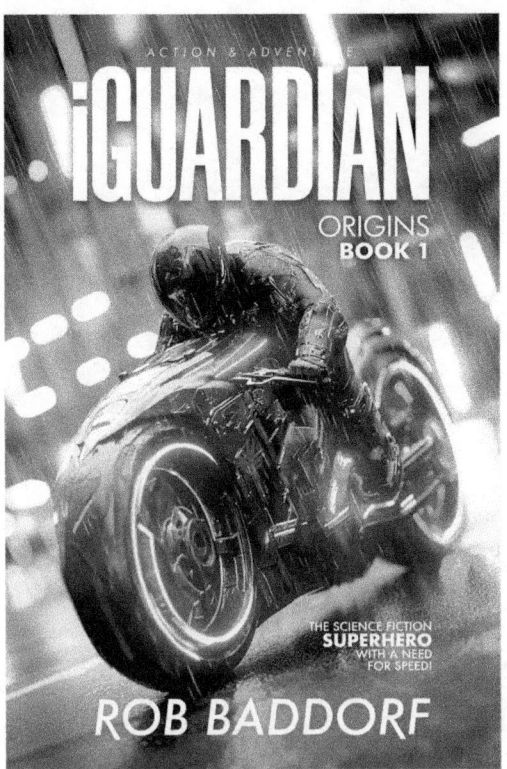

ACTION & ADVENTURE

iGUARDIAN

ORIGINS
BOOK 1

THE SCIENCE FICTION
SUPERHERO
WITH A NEED
FOR SPEED!

ROB BADDORF

**A wild ride. A transforming machine.
A teen with nothing to lose but his fear.**

Noah didn't mean to become a hero—he just saw someone in trouble and jumped in to help. Now, he's caught the attention of a secret organization with a crazy offer: test-drive a next-gen vehicle that can shift, adapt, and pull off stunts no one else can. Fly past traffic? Done. Dive underwater? No problem. Stick to the tunnel ceiling? Absolutely.

With a cutting-edge machine at his fingertips and a team backing him from the shadows, Noah finds himself racing into danger to help others in need. Each mission is more daring than the last—but this time, he's not alone, and he's not just a kid with guts. He's the pilot of something game-changing.

4 Book Series!

When Andrew and Kate are pushed off their screens and out of their bedrooms for two weeks, they discover an enchanted meadow. But who will survive their exile the longest?

Grounded from screens and bored out of their minds, Andrew and Kate stumble onto a mysterious farmer's scavenger hunt that leads them deep into the woods—and toward an enchanted meadow.

There, they strike a deal: whoever can last two weeks without their old comforts wins. But as they discover unexpected treasures, both must decide what "winning" really means—and whether they can share the riches they've found.

3 Book Series!